VALEDICTORY

Daniel Scott

Savant Books and Publications
Honolulu, HI, USA
2015

Daniel Scott

Published in the USA by Savant Books and Publications
2630 Kapiolani Blvd #1601
Honolulu, HI 96826
http://www.savantbooksandpublications.com

Printed in the USA

Edited by Suzanne Langford
Cover Art and Design by Jessica Orfe

13-digit ISBN: 9780991562299

For Dennis

Daniel Scott

PART I

April 20, 1988

Daniel Scott

1

Earl Castle slipped the book bag off his shoulder and let it drop. He pressed his back to the concrete wall and slowly slid downward until he felt the grimy linoleum floor through the seat of his black denim jeans.

Directly across the corridor was his professor's office, locked up, no light showing under the door. She was supposed to meet him more than four hours ago.

Anyone else would have given up and gone home, but Earl possessed an iron single-mindedness the temper of which almost no one suspected.

From the first day he walked onto the campus of the Municipal University of New York, he said, out loud to no one, "I will be the valedictorian of my class."

He was not sure how or from where the idea came to him. He was certainly not in any way driven to succeed at the vocational high school on Long Island he drowsed through for four years.

He was just weeks from graduation and perhaps days from finding out if he had cleared the first major hurdle he had set for himself as part of The Great Plan—he thought of it that way oftentimes, with even the article capitalized. And he'd be closer to knowing if only his professor had cared enough to show up for their appointment.

He opened his eyes without realizing he had ever shut them. He began to think that going home might be the most prudent thing to do at this point. Exhaustion was starting to rack him, and among the knowledge he'd gained in his time at Municipal University was that he risked doing stupid things when he was exhausted, even things that undermined the progress of The Great Plan.

But as Earl got up to go, he halted.

His professor was coming right at him, looking a little unstable on her legs. He saw that she had taken off her shoes, and her nyloned feet were causing her to slip on the linoleum floor.

She carried a stack of books and manila envelopes stuffed with papers and a large pocketbook with a Navajo design on it swung from her shoulder.

She took no notice of Earl until she got near him, and even then she seemed not to recognize him. In an instant though, her eyes rolled almost completely into her head and she muttered, "Shit."

"Hello, Professor Rasmussen-Vell," Earl said. At all times he addressed her and all his teachers in this way: "Professor" followed by the last name exactly as it appeared on the syllabus. Never before had it been such an awkward mouthful. Maybe that was why she implored her students to call her "Sonia."

She fished for her keys in her pocketbook. Earl glimpsed inside and saw the soft scuffed sneakers she had taken off.

"We were supposed to have a conference...?" he said.

"I know, Earl."

He had never been so close to her before. He had never noticed the strands of silver in her faded chestnut mane, or how the skin around her knuckles wrinkled as she fussed with the keys.

She unlocked the door to reveal the closet-sized space she shared with the two other teachers whose hours were taped to the door alongside hers.

A desk had been wedged in so that when she sat down at it her back was to whoever was visiting her. The drawers were marred by the remains of peeled-off stickers. A clear plastic cup for pens and pencils was bolted to the desktop. Chained to that was a stapler with a PROPERTY OF MUNICIPAL U. label on it.

The only thing that indicated the office was in any way hers was the small cassette player sitting above the desk on a single shelf of unshellacked wood. Now and then she played music on it in class to "set the tone" for the day's theme, though to Earl she never fully succeeded in linking the ideas in the music with her topics. He always thought she was just filling up time.

She swiveled around.

"So, Earl," she said, "what is it you want so bad that you waited all this time for?" A strange question for her, though not because she ended it with a superfluous preposition.

"You know, if this is a bad time, I could come

back…"

"For God's sake we're here now, Earl. What do you want?"

He tried to get a hold on what he needed to do. The way to play this was calm and respectful, earnest and eager to do better.

"It's about the paper you handed back today."

"What about it?"

"I can't tell what the grade is."

"You can't tell?"

He truly could not.

He produced the paper from his book bag and handed it to her. The more he had stared at the grade etched in red pen on the upper right corner of the first page, the more it became some kind of alien calligraphy with no recognizable meaning. There were otherwise no comments on the paper. No "Nice" or "Good point" or "Couldn't you have expanded on this more?"

There were no signs that the thing had actually been read.

Normally that wouldn't bother Earl, but that grade there… A? A-? B? The uncertainty, and what it might mean for The Great Plan, had shaken him. He despaired when she refused to talk with him right after class, saying she had three minutes to be on the other side of campus. He had to slip into a men's room stall and stay there until his heart slowed down and he could stop sweating.

Rasmussen squinted at it. She said, "You can't read this?"

"It's just a little hard to make out," said Earl.

She handed it back.

"It's a B."

Something softened in her as her eyes failed to meet his.

"It was a very good paper."

A muteness overcame him.

"A B is a perfectly good grade, Earl. Most students would be happy to get a grade like that."

He looked at the floor. He didn't want her to see the ferocity behind his eyes. He didn't want her to know that he was not interested in what would make most students happy. He was sure if she knew that, she would never be persuaded to change the grade.

He took a deep, silent breath and said, "I'd like to do better. Maybe I could rewrite the paper. Do some extra credit…"

She laughed. It was not a big laugh, but, for chrissake, she was laughing at him.

She spoke in a voice that sounded nothing like the timid, tentative bleat Earl had come to hate over the past two-and-a-half months.

"What you're really saying is you want an A, right? What you're really saying is that since you got a B on the only paper required for the course, you're afraid you'll get a B for the final grade, right? Or did you think I was too stupid to figure that out?"

She leaned back and the chair squeaked underneath her.

Earl stayed composed. He kept The Plan in his sights.

"I don't know why you would say that," he said. "And I don't understand why you would have a problem with a student trying to get an A in your class."

"And why is that so important to you, Earl? Don't tell me. You have a perfect 4.0 GPA and you don't want to mess it up, right?"

He couldn't deny that she was right about that.

"Do you have any idea how many people have four-O's in this ridiculous school, Earl? Do you really think getting all A's is so hard to do here? You're a bright student, I know, Earl, but you're competing with the absolute bottom of the barrel!"

Earl's stoicism did not change. Her words, though unusual for her, were nothing he hadn't heard in various other ways from various other people inside and outside Muni. Maybe he'd even said them to himself once or twice. But he knew that if, for instance, he had only a 3.9 GPA, those very same people would be griping that he couldn't get a 4.0 even at Muni.

He would have been all too happy to lump Professor Rasmussen-Vell in with those people, but he couldn't just yet. She still had to be made to change the grade.

The task would be more difficult than he first thought.

"I don't think any of that means I shouldn't try to do my best," he said in a low, husky voice.

She looked down at her lap. He thought he saw her nod a little, and then she sighed. It sounded like she was deflating.

"So, is there a possibility I could do the paper over...?"

"Even if I did give you an A on the paper," she said, "that would be no guarantee of anything. Final grades are based on more than just that. There's other things. Class participation, for instance."

Earl could hardly believe what he was hearing. Had she been totally oblivious to the countless times over the semester when it was his "class participation" that rescued her from making a complete ass of herself?

This must have dawned on her after she said it because she quickly added, "There's also collegiality…"

Earl nodded like he understood but he was really wondering how this could have happened, how his fate could have slipped from his own control into the hands of this person, how he could have misread her so disastrously. Maybe he had extended himself too far, as he had been warned against doing. Maybe somewhere along the way he should have taken off at least one summer semester.

"I've noticed that you don't socialize very much with the other students, Earl. You don't mix."

He understood that he did not so much impress

people as impress upon them.

"And I've noticed you always sit in the chair closest to the exit. And that when class ends, you're always the first one out the door."

He was the type of person people did not like to do things for. He was the type who had to earn everything.

"Earl…?"

"I'm sorry," he said. "I guess I didn't realize I was doing something wrong."

She backpedaled in her chair, bumping the desk behind her. She pulled herself up straight.

"Sometimes I get the feeling you think my class is some kind of joke," she said in a softer voice.

That surprised him. He'd done everything he could not to convey that.

"I don't think that," he said. "I mean, I think your class is very interesting."

"Really?"

"I feel like I learned a lot."

"Well. I'm glad." Only she didn't sound glad. She sounded like she didn't believe him. It wasn't clear if she didn't believe him because he was obviously lying, or because she doubted anyone could learn a lot in her class.

She spun around, propped her elbows on the desk, and rested her forehead in her hands.

"You'll have to go now, Earl," she said. "I have some things I have to do."

But Earl couldn't leave. He couldn't even move. He croaked that there must be something he could do.

"There isn't, Earl."

"Maybe you can give me an incomplete. I could put off graduating for a year. I could retake the course…"

"You'd be willing to do that?" She was turned away from him but Earl could still read the disgust on her face.

"Yes. If I have to."

"I'm sorry, Earl. I'm afraid that won't be possible."

"It could be possible if you'd just say yes."

"No, Earl."

"It's not right," he said, his temper tipping over. "It's not right of you to do this simply because you don't like me!"

"No, it's not. Now if you'll excuse me…"

"Maybe I could…"

She shot to her feet.

"The B stands, Earl! Now please leave! Or do I have to have to call security?"

He backed away to the door. She surely knew that any dustups with security would sink him at the school forever.

Before he left, he said, "Have a nice evening, Professor Rasmussen-Vell."

At first all Earl could do was stumble forward, down the same corridors he'd roamed all afternoon, and for the last four years. He'd been moving forward so long, progressing and advancing, that it had become an instinct.

He pushed open a set of double doors that led to a stairwell and dropped himself on the cement steps.

He pressed his face against the steel cage that shot up the middle of the stairwell from bottom floor to top. He began shaking and sweating.

Perhaps there had been valedictorians with 3.9's or even 3.8's. But those were students with other attributes to push. They were cryptically pretty young women who organized food drives in Central America, or visibly foreign young men who survived earthquakes or tyrants or several days at sea to be there.

In other words, there was something morally superior about them. They were engaged with the world in ways that aimed to make it a better place. And that made up for that tiny lack of robot efficiency.

Earl had no such eminence and no such lack. Not being naturally deserving, he had to earn it.

The only thing he knew how to do was work harder than anyone else, work the world into submission, until he got what he wanted.

He decided he would go talk to her again.

But first, he needed to get himself calm.

Daniel Scott

2

He strapped his book bag back on and took another stride around the fourth floor of the Fripp Academic Building, but at a slower pace than he'd been walking it for the past few hours.

Fripp was the main venue for classes at the Municipal University of New York, which was commonly called "Muni." The building was a four-story glass square. The insides of the corridors were the entryways to the classrooms, offices, electrical closets, and maintenance rooms. The outsides were the floor-to-ceiling glass windowpanes that looked out over the red-brick campus. It was a relatively recent addition to what was a genuine institution in the city, one supposedly referred to as "the Harvard of the proletariat." In his four years there, Earl never heard anyone say any such thing.

The classrooms he passed along the east corridor, mainly for freshman survey courses, were alternately deserted and overflowing into the hallway. The outliers strained their necks to hear their professors.

The south corridor was monopolized by the English Department except for a single office shared by the Departments of Jewish Studies and Romance Languages, according to a piece of paper taped to the door.

A small segment of the glass wall in the west corridor was given over to a succession of corkboards for posters and notices. Earl had had the time to study every flyer tacked thereon.

Help with English and math was available on a walk-in basis at the Student Advisement Center.

A charity basketball game featuring some hip-hop artists and deejays from the neighborhood could be attended (though the flyer didn't specify just what the good cause was) for five dollars a ticket with a Muni ID, seven without.

The Muni Gay and Lesbian Coalition was doing something, but the flier had been ripped down except for the part with their letterhead.

And then there was the day-glo pink sheet of paper put up by Dr. Henry Althus, the head of the History Department's Black Studies program. DISTRIBUTORS WANTED, it read. He was looking to market videotapes and cassettes of himself speechifying. The topics weren't revealed but more than likely included the same ones that had recently made Henry Althus a notorious figure on campus and throughout the city. He proffered theories that included references to dark-skinned "sun people" who had naturally warm and communal ways and pale "ice people" who were cold and out for themselves. At least that was as far as Earl was willing to delve. He, of course, had a low tolerance for idiocy and, besides, as a pale person, he felt rather slighted.

Across from the flyers, through the glass wall, the sideways sunlight of the late afternoon made the place look unfamiliar to Earl. He had always taken the earliest classes possible, indicative of his desire to get in and get it done—or, lately, just get it over with.

Lights were beginning to flicker around the Administration Building's small cement plaza, with its bolted-down benches and two small leafy trees.

One of them laid snapped at the base and dangling over the side of the dirt-filled cement basin it was planted in.

There had been a student protest the day before. The governor was raising tuition and still making cutbacks in staff and resources. Earl had glimpsed the commotion as he was rushing to his seminar on Lyndon Johnson. The protesters marched from the Kirsch Science Building to Administration, chanting and carrying signs with big red numbers purporting to show the annual salaries of the college president and the chancellor. Somehow, in the midst of it all, the tree was felled.

Last night Earl had seen the brief mention of it on the news his grandfather Bertram was watching. There were conflicting accounts of how the tree came down. A young black woman identified as a student said some protesters climbed it to get a view into the president's second-floor office. A middle-aged white man said to be a university official said they were identifying those involved, and that they could face charges for destruction of school property as well as academic disciplinary action. The police were called, but made no arrests.

"Every time Muni makes the news, it's for something bad!" Bertram had said.

"Could you turn that down a little?" Earl said. "I'm trying to study."

"When I went to Muni, we had pride. We protested when we had to, but we didn't destroy the campus. We didn't look to all the world like a bunch of savages!"

Earl was grateful to Bertram for giving him a rent-free place to live while he went to school, but he had long since had his fill of the old man's opinions, especially where Muni was concerned.

Bertram watched the screen with his pimpled forearms crossed tightly against his chest.

"When I went there, you had to be smart to get in. You had to take a test! They didn't take just any bum with a Pell grant. And that's another thing: when I went there, it was free! People called it The Free Academy."

"I thought you said they called it the Harvard of the proletariat?" Earl said.

"They did! They called it both!"

To Bertram, his beloved alma mater had gone

from an approximation of the Ivy League to proof of the downfall of American education. Obviously he preferred it when the student body consisted of mostly white, Jewish, impecunious young intellectuals. Today's proletarians were just as broke, but they were no longer just whites.

They were blacks.

They were Latinos from almost every country in the hemisphere.

In smaller numbers they were Chinese and Japanese and Koreans, and in sprinklings East Europeans, Arabs, Africans, French, and others.

Bertram was right about one thing: Muni had suffered through a terrible streak of bad luck that seemed to begin just as Earl's freshman year did.

The most attention-grabbing was the videotape of a rambling Althus that had found its way onto one of those new public-access channels that had started popping up in Manhattan.

For a time Earl couldn't arrive on campus without spotting a TV news van or someone with a tape recorder interviewing people and nodding a lot.

There were outraged calls for Althus' dismissal.

Protesters egged his home in Hoboken.

The mayor was forced to chime in, saying he should step down but that it was really an internal university matter. The board of regents and the college president disavowed Althus' statements.

The New York Times wrote an editorial that never exactly called for his resignation, but which left that very strong impression.

In the end, nothing of consequence happened. Althus was well entrenched, protected by tenure, the First Amendment, and a cadre of loyalist-students who defended his views as well as his person.

Earl detested the man for making Muni look so bad, but he had to admit he was impressed with his ability to persevere.

Two years later and Bertram still brought it up whenever he could.

"That's where open admissions gets you," he had said. "That killed Muni right there. You think I'm just an old man talking."

"Less obvious is how I'm going to finish this reading before my class in the morning," said Earl.

So Bertram leaned forward and turned down the TV volume, saying he could watch the TV in his room. The quest for academic furtherance was something he respected a great deal.

As Earl looked at the tree now through the glass wall, he wondered, too, how long it would take the school to repair it, or at least remove it.

The clock atop Administration read five past five, which Earl knew meant twenty-five past five.

He walked on slowly, turning at the north corridor, where Rasmussen's office was. He stopped and took some deep breaths. Then he proceeded to the office door. He thought he saw a flash of some sort down around his feet. Then he noticed there was no light coming from under her door.

Still he knocked, softly at first, then harder.

"Professor Rasmussen-Vell?"

Finally he stepped back.

He mulled his options.

He could go over her head, to whom he wasn't sure. Only students in academic peril knew things like that.

He wondered if Calvin had gone home yet.

3

Calvin Reynolds had been going to Muni on and off, full-time and part-time, for more than six years, supposedly majoring in education while also working in the small office adjacent to the History chairman's. Mostly he answered phones and sorted the mail. But his greatest usefulness was that he seemed to know everything that went on at the school, simply because he'd been there so long.

Earl found Calvin at his desk with the phone cradled between his chin and shoulder and a clipboard gripped in his hands. He looked up at Earl. His moist eyes, a few shades of brown darker than his skin, were framed by round metal-rimmed glasses. His short black bristly beard always reminded Earl of a G.I. Joe doll he had as a boy.

"Look," he was saying into the phone, "now is a really bad time to talk." Calvin may have been the closest Earl had come to making a friend at Muni, but they were still just casual enough acquaintances to have no secrets. Earl wondered why there was suddenly something Calvin could not discuss in his presence.

Calvin hung up the phone and said, "I can't go for a cigarette right now, Earl. I have too much to do here."

"Going for a cigarette" was their euphemism for sneaking off to the maintenance room one floor down.

"Actually I just came to ask you a question," Earl said.

"Oh." Calvin nodded toward the small hardwood chair next to his desk. "You'll have to make it fast."

"I need to know how a student would go about protesting a grade," said Earl.

Calvin narrowed his eyes. "Protesting a grade?" he said.

"Yeah. If a student thinks a teacher gave him the wrong grade, what can the student do?"

"You're having trouble with grades?" Calvin said.

"Just one. This professor—she's unbelievable —she wants to screw me over just because it's the one little bit of power she has in her rotten life."

Calvin chuckled. Berating the professors was something he would never have dared, or could ever have afforded.

"Well, you'd have to file an official grievance first," Calvin said. "You'd have to explain in writing why you think you deserve a better grade. Then there'd be some sort of meeting between you and the teacher and a mediator."

It sounded to Earl terribly involved.

"Would this go on my record in any kind of official way?" he wanted to know.

"It could. Especially if the professor decides to really fight you on it. But what you really have to worry about is the gossip between the professors. If it gets around that you're some kind of hard case, that could hurt you more than anything."

"What would you say my chances of winning are?"

"Did this teacher flunk you?"

"She gave me a B."

"Oh. So it's this A-or-nothin' thing you got going."

"Yeah."

Calvin may not have considered himself privileged, but he was the only person Earl had ever told about The Great Plan.

"Well, nine times out of ten the university will back the professor. If they admit a professor made a mistake, it makes it look they were the ones who made the mistake, and they have the board of regents to answer to. And things are very tense right now, with the budget cuts coming down. I don't suppose you were at the protest yesterday?"

"So you're saying the chances are not good."

"I'm saying that, in your case, with your record, you might have a real shot. Did you see how we knocked that tree over?"

"You did that?"

"Yup. See this?" He showed a long but mild scrape on his forearm. "I got this when I hit the ground."

"So you guys tore it down on purpose?"

"No. That's what the school wants everyone to think. The tree just snapped and came down. Sometimes things happen in a protest, you know?"

The first time Earl ever saw Calvin, he was outside the main entrance of Fripp amid the students as they streamed in and out, spinning like a traffic cop as he passed out copies of *The Black & Brown Liberator* from a sack on his shoulder.

His handsome radiance was enough to cause Earl to stop and stare. Calvin was thickly built but the thickness was stretched over a tall and wide frame. He wore jeans that looked faded and comfortable, allowing the easy grace of his body to come through. Earl saw him intermittently after that, always from a distance, and always left momentarily disabled by the lust aroused in him. He could hardly believe it when almost three years later the same man, perhaps even in the same jeans, showed up in the shadowy stacks of Muntsen Library's little-visited top floor, an area where men sometimes cruised for sex.

"So would you say I had a better than fifty percent chance?" Earl said.

"I really couldn't give you a number, Earl," said Calvin.

He glanced at the pie-sized clock on the office wall. He reached under his desk and pulled out a styrofoam cooler. It was packed with bottles of beer, but no ice.

"Don't look at me like that," he said. "These are for the end-of-the-semester party the department has. It's past office hours now. I've been working late a lot lately. I deserve it."

"I wasn't looking at you in any way, Calvin."

"You want one?"

Earl was not much on drinking. He had seen and dismissed the puerile fascination with getting drunk that seemed to preoccupy almost everyone he knew while he was growing up—his mother, her friends, the kids he went to high school with. Besides, he was not a big guy like Calvin but actually rather slight, and it didn't take a lot of alcohol to affect him adversely.

Then again, he found himself not wanting to refuse something that came from Calvin.

To his surprise, warm beer wasn't quite as revolting as cold. He could at least let it down his throat without visibly shuddering.

"You know," Calvin said, "sometimes you can work these things out if you just sit down and talk to the professor. I mean, most of the time, teachers try to be helpful to their students. Mine have always been to me."

"That's because you're you," Earl said. "And don't look at me like that." Indeed, Calvin was one of those people who was genuinely liked. "Besides, I already tried talking to her. It made things worse."

Calvin laughed. It was not lost on Earl that when he sat back with his beer he kept his legs open, or that his free hand dangled now in the vicinity of his crotch. Earl could tell what was coming.

"Maybe I do have time for a quick cigarette," Calvin said, as if Earl had really come for that in the first place.

Earl's exhaustion and despair were weighing on him, and the beer was making him a little nauseous, but his desire for Calvin was never very far away, and it did not take much for him to summon it.

"This might be the last chance we get to do this," Calvin smiled.

"Why is that?" Earl said.

"You're graduating in a few weeks, right?"

"Oh. I suppose."

"And you're not gonna come back to Muni in

the fall just to get it on with me, are you?"

"I suppose not."

Their primary trysting place, to which Calvin had a key, contained a stack of old gym mats well-situated behind a wall of unused metal shelving. Two people could lay down on it if they wanted.

Calvin locked up the office.

As usual, Earl stayed a few steps behind as they headed one flight down the stairwell and emerged on the second floor. Calvin had told him to finish his beer before they left. Earl became inflamed as he watched Calvin's slightly off-center butt resist the grab of his jeans.

When Calvin reached the maintenance room, he walked straight past it and stopped at the bulletin boards. Earl meanwhile stopped at the door and unlocked it, having been given the key. He left the key in the lock and disappeared inside. This had become their usual mode of operation. Ostensibly they were fooling the world about what they were up to.

Earl was greeted by the familiar stale stink of old mops standing in rusty three-wheeled pails. Along the wall were several floor buffers, a stack of filters for oil furnaces, a dented and grime-covered bullhorn.

The only illumination was the red bulb on the wall next to the fire extinguisher and the glowing EXIT sign over the door.

He went behind the metal shelves to the pile of gym mats, which rose knee-high. Typically Earl sat on them and serviced the standing Calvin from there. He took his place and waited.

Sex was one of the few pleasures Earl allowed himself. He unbuckled his belt and started to rub himself in anticipation. His lids sank halfway over his eyes. His body felt light, almost as if he could float if he wanted.

The EXIT sign dimmed with the opening of the door and brightened again at the closing. He listened as Calvin shook the door to make sure it was locked.

But Calvin didn't step up and start unbuckling, as Earl expected. Instead he went over to a large plastic trashcan that stood by the shelves. He removed the lid and dug through a lot of crumpled-up copies of *The Liberator*, and pulled out a brown bottle. Earl chuckled. "Is that for the end-of-the-semester party too?"

"Could be. You want one?"

Again, he did not want to say no to Calvin.

Calvin twisted both caps off at the same time, muffling the sound in his hand. He sat next to Earl on the mats, which he almost never did before the sex. He lifted his bottle for a toast, and Earl knew there was something different about Calvin on this day.

"Here's to changes," Calvin said. He nearly knocked the bottle from Earl's hand when they clinked. He downed half the beer in the first swig.

"Let's burn one," he said. He shook out two cigarettes from the pack in his shirt pocket, handing one to Earl. He lit his own with a match and then blew it out. He leaned in close toward Earl and the tips of their cigarettes touched, one transferring its fire to the one that was not lit.

Earl wasn't much of a smoker either. He drew more deeply than he intended, coughed, and his head began to swim.

"Big changes are coming," Calvin couldn't resist saying again. He had a way of holding his beer by just the neck of the bottle, with a deft rigging of three of his fingers. "Very soon."

On occasion their ten-minute interludes in the

maintenance room stretched to a half-hour or more. This only happened when Calvin was feeling talkative, and the more he drank, the more he talked.

It was in this way that Earl learned most of what he knew about Calvin's life outside Muni. He'd been married at nineteen and divorced by twenty-one. He had no relationship with his daughter even though she only lived over in Jersey City. She would start junior high in the fall and thought of another man as her father. Calvin didn't carry a picture of her, but he did have pictures, he said.

Earl managed to slip in some information about himself during these times. He heard himself saying perfectly ordinary things that he had nevertheless not said to anyone before, that he shared an apartment on West 83rd Street with his grandfather who was not really his grandfather but his step-grandfather but who wasn't even that now that his grandmother was dead. Any such autobiography, however, was always met by Calvin with a drag from a cigarette, a swig of a beer and a failure to ask Earl for any elaboration.

Except for the time Earl revealed to him The

Great Plan. For that Calvin sat there forgetting to blink. Earl wondered if Calvin's rapt attention made him tell more than he should have.

So Calvin knew about Earl's distortedly raging desire to get all A's, be valedictorian, and win a full scholarship from the Rhyman Foundation for History and Politics, which would allow him two years of graduate school overseas, spending a semester each in various European capitals. It jibed perfectly with Earl's major—International Politics—but that wasn't the only reason he wanted it so badly.

"So you have things pretty well planned out," Calvin had said when Earl first told him about The Plan.

"I do," said Earl.

"And what if you don't get the full scholarship from Rhyman?"

"I will. If I'm valedictorian. Which will only happen if my GPA stays a 4.0."

"But that won't guarantee you getting a scholarship."

"Not by itself, no. But I also have an in at Rhyman."

"A what?"

"An in."

"You mean you know someone there who's in a position to help you."

"But I have to live up to my end of the bargain first," Earl said.

Calvin thought a moment.

"And what is it you hope to accomplish by all of this?" he said.

Earl smiled. "To get away."

"From what?"

"Everything. My family. New York. I'd like to get away from the person I can't help being when I'm here." It wasn't by solely professional reasons that Earl was driven, but also by a private desire to start afresh, to stop being the person he had been defined to be. When he got right down to it, not even Earl liked Earl very much.

Calvin eyed him skeptically and said, "Uh-huh."

Earl could never tell what Calvin thought about The Great Plan because Calvin never expressed an opinion about it. In the two years since he first told him about it, he never even mentioned it unless Earl brought it up.

But Earl had long since learned to accept

Calvin's reticence about matters of feeling. In fact it helped keep their relationship mysterious and alluring.

Earl reached over and squeezed Calvin's crotch.

Calvin said, "Hold on there. That's not going anywhere."

Calvin jumped up to get another beer, and one for Earl as well. It was Earl's third, or possibly fourth. By now the alcohol was going down easier. It was almost like drinking water.

"You know about the tuition hike, right?" Calvin said, plopping down again.

"Mmmm…"

"What's the matter with you?"

"Nothing. Tell me about the changes…" He tried to focus as Calvin expounded the latest crisis to grip the campus of The Municipal University of New York.

Crises revisited the school so faithfully that a palpable sense of the apocalyptic sometimes stalked the halls and classrooms.

This was the second time tuition had gone up since Earl had been at Muni. Someone raised a stink about it then, as he recalled, but the cost went up anyway and the betrayal by the university of its own proclaimed mission to educate the poor never really showed itself.

"The purpose of the hike," Calvin was saying, "is to drive the most disadvantaged students out of the university. Did you hear what the chancellor said?"

At this point Earl was not really following along. He was looking at Calvin and thinking again of his G.I. Joe doll of long ago. He remembered dunking it underwater once and the soft fuzzy beard fell out. He never played with it again after that.

"We're not gonna stand for that," Calvin said.

"Oh," said Earl. He was riding a fluttery feeling that seemed to emanate from his chest. "What are we gonna do?"

"We?" Calvin said. "Are you drunk?"

"No. Tell me everything, Calvin."

Calvin eyed him. He finished off the beer. "Nah."

"Tell me."

"I can't. You don't really care anyway."

"What? I care…"

Calvin laughed. He hopped up and started

unbuckling himself. He looked down at Earl, who was smiling at him rather dreamily.

"We're doing this, right?" Calvin said.

"Oh." Earl polished off the beer. "Yeah."

Calvin luxuriated in the sex a little more than usual, even allowing himself to moan as he was being serviced. In the course of it Earl slipped from the mats to his knees on the floor.

He was a good bit sloppier than usual, but he got the job done just as well. It always felt good to give himself over to someone's gratification other than his own.

When it was over, Earl pulled himself up, but a sharp spasm made him fall forward onto the mats.

"What's the matter with you?" Calvin said.

"It's my knee." A ridge in the pocked cement floor had worked its way under his kneecap, making it impossible to straighten his right leg.

"You gonna be alright?"

"I suppose." He laid back on the mats and began to think his larger problem was the room he was in, how it lagged behind his vision wherever he turned his head. Perhaps more pressing than that was a starting stir of nausea.

Calvin looked at his watch. "I gotta get back."

He started buckling up. "Hey, don't fall asleep!"

"I'm not..." Earl said, "...you stupid..."

"What did you call me?"

"Not you. That fucking Rasmussen."

"Rasmussen's the teacher you're having problems with?" Calvin said. "Sonia Rasmussen?"

"You know her?"

"Of course," he said. "You might have a really good shot, considering it's her."

"Really?"

"She's in trouble here. She's up for tenure and the word is she's not getting it. The meeting was supposed to be today, I think. Six years she's taught here. And now they're giving her the heave-ho."

Earl hated that he couldn't grasp things as quickly as he normally could. "You're saying they're firing her?"

"They say she hasn't published enough. But that's not the real reason. The real reason is she's not liked."

"That must have been why she was acting so crazy," Earl said.

"Crazy how?"

"Screaming. Telling me being valedictorian at

Muni was nothing."

"Sounds like your case is getting stronger all the time." Calvin tucked in his shirt. "Listen, pull yourself together. If you need a minute that's okay. Just don't forget to pull the door all the way shut on your way out."

"Where are you going, Calvin?"

"I gotta get back. Just make the sure the door is locked when you leave, okay?"

"Okay."

"And listen, if we never see each other again, good luck with your big plan or whatever."

"Calvin?"

"What?"

"I hope…I mean…maybe…"

"Are you gonna be alright?"

"Yeah."

Earl watched the EXIT sign dim as Calvin left, then brighten again with the closing of the door. He closed his eyes.

4

Bertram Berg was accustomed to eating alone but not to being the only one in the apartment come suppertime.

By now, usually, Earl would have been holed up in his room for several hours, studying or listening to that racket he called music or doing whatever else he did in there.

Bertram carried the dishes to the sink and washed them right away. He had lived alone most of his life and never really grew used to having a wife pick up after him. Even during the five glorious years when he was married to Earl's grandmother Jo, he was the one who did the chores.

He took in the living room as he patted his hands dry with the dishtowel. Inevitably his eyes came to rest on the small vessel of white-frosted glass that sat on a stand by the door. It had been a gift from Jo's daughter Colleen—Earl's mother—on the occasion of Jo and Bertram's marriage. It had a thin gold rim. They were perplexed at what to do with it. It was too deep to be a bowl, not deep enough to be a vase.

Bertram had forgotten about it until, almost a year after her funeral, he decided to face the task of cleaning out Jo's closet.

Earl was moving in, after all, and he needed the space for his things.

"What is it your mother thought this thing was supposed to be used for?" he had said to Earl. He was kneeling on the floor of the closet and holding up the wedding gift in one hand.

"You're supposed to just leave it around for other people to gawk at," Earl had said. "She has things like that all over the house. Ugly as they are useless. Like her."

"Don't talk down your mother, Earl. It makes people question your character."

Bertram decided to put it where it was now and it became the place on top of which he left any mail that came addressed to Earl.

A letter had arrived today, in fact: "From the Office of the Dean of The Municipal University of New York."

All afternoon Bertram had been waiting for Earl to come home and open it.

He would have loved nothing better than to tear into it immediately. But he had to restrain himself from interfering in Earl's business.

The thing was, though, while he was very proud of Earl and very glad to be of help to him, Earl hardly ever told him anything.

Bertram traced that silence to an afternoon just after the start of Earl's junior year when he let his curiosity best his common sense and he opened a final grade report that had shown up in the mail. Earl walked in to find the old man sitting at the dining room table, the paper in his hand, tears brimming in his eyes.

"Earl," he had said, "why didn't you tell me?"

"I told you I was doing alright!" said Earl, who bristled at every intrusion of Bertram's.

"You're doing better than alright!" Bertram said. "You're doing the best you could possibly be doing! Look at this. A, A, A. A. A, A, A. A. A. I'm so proud of you, Earl!"

Earl snatched the paper from his hands.

"Look," he said, "I'm really grateful to you for everything, but don't ever open my mail again!"

He didn't exactly storm off then, nor did he really slam his bedroom door. But somehow Bertram knew it was that mistake that pushed Earl, who had always been somewhat reticent, to make a point of keeping things to himself.

Thank God, though, that Muni was too strapped to afford envelopes that could not be seen through when held up to a light bulb.

Bertram's eyes may not have been as sharp as they were in the days when he scrutinized actuarial tables for a living, but he could make out "Dear...Mr...Castle."

A formal salutation like that. Nothing like it had ever come for Earl before. At least not as far as Bertram knew.

He put the letter on the table and picked up the phone. It was a touch-tone, and he punched the numbers on the pad like he was using an adding machine.

"I'm worried about the kid," he said to his friend, Walt Escher. "He hasn't come home yet."

"Ah, Bert," said Walt. "You sound like a

mother hen."

"I'm not that. But I'm worried, you know, with the school being in such a lousy neighborhood."

"You probably haven't even been up there in the hundred years since you and I went to the place."

"I've been to Harlem many times since then."

"You have not."

"And anyway Earl's no city kid like you and I were."

"Don't worry about him, Bert. Maybe he met a girl and got himself laid. It would probably do him some good."

"That didn't happen. You know his schoolwork is too important to him to get involved with any of that nonsense."

"Yeah I know."

"Especially now, so close to graduation…" He was tracing with his finger the seal of the envelope. "I'd hate to see him screw it all up at this late stage."

"Me too, Bert."

"Have you talked to the people at Rhyman yet?"

"The best time for me to get involved is after

Earl submits all of his documentation. Especially his transcript. Especially if he gets all A's again this semester and makes valedictorian. After that, we'll see."

Walt was once close friends with the Institute's namesake, Marcus Rhyman, an old Muni classmate who, like Walt, had launched into better things.

Bertram knew they had a falling-out years later over something or other. He asked Walt about it once, and Walt dismissed it as a matter of no importance. Bertram was left to his own suspicions. He knew Rhyman had married and divorced a very attractive woman.

The rift was patched up after Marcus ceased to live. He was driving on I-95 outside New Haven one evening when the snow began to really pile up. He got off at the next exit and parked at a gas station under the overpass, figuring he'd wait it out. He went into the convenience store to get a paper and when he came out, there was a loud crash overhead. A car had skidded off the overpass, smashed through the railing and landed right on top of him.

Walt spoke at his funeral.

"Don't get your hopes unreasonably high, Bert," he said. "The fact that Earl's from Muni will be a strike against him."

"But with you pulling for him, he can't lose," said Bertram.

"That's not really the way it works, Bert."

Bertram was never sure why people like Walt always downplayed the influence they had over other people.

"If Earl was chosen, they would contact him by letter, wouldn't they?" Bertram said.

"I would think," said Walt. "Although it is Muni. They do do everything ass backwards. First, though, they'd contact him for an interview."

"By letter?"

Walt went silent on the line. Then he said, "Don't do it, Bert."

"Do what?"

"Don't open the letter."

"What letter?"

"You remember how angry he was last time? He had every right to be, too."

"Nothing like that is going on. I better get off the phone now, in case he's trying to call."

"He's entitled to a little privacy, Bert."

"Goodbye, Walt."

"Goodbye, Bert."

Bertram felt a little entitled himself.

The kid after all was staying in his apartment rent-free. He was eating his food.

Not that Bertram really minded or couldn't afford it.

But that wasn't the point.

Of course, Walt was right. He was one of those tedious people who were always right. That was obvious the first time Bertram laid eyes on Walter Escher, in 1938, a time when The Municipal University fairly crackled with discourse deeply concerned about who was right and who was wrong. It wasn't so much the classrooms that heard the debate as it was the enormous first-floor cafeteria, and especially the alcoves that lined one side of it. The alcove one chose to sit at advertised where one stood on the pressing issues of the day. The Communists and anti-Stalinists were the biggest groups, and accordingly they took their places in alcoves one and two. But down the line there were many others factions with names like Ohlerites and Marlinites and Lovestonites—each an invocation of a purported thinker whom, they each fervently believed, made all the others look like charlatans.

As dynamic as all that was, most of the students ate at the large rectangular communal tables that filled the rest of the cafeteria while talking about more mundane things—classes, professors, women, movies. They were there not to change the world but simply to fit themselves into it somewhere. They had come to get equipped with formal educations in order to conduct lives that were successful and satisfying according to the prescriptions of those who brought them up.

Bertram was, at this time, one of this vast majority. The murky concerns of the alcove dwellers—didn't they ever to go to class?—were not his. Still, depending on where he sat, he sometimes caught an earful of them. Walt Escher was the hottest of the firebrands, and the hardest to ignore.

Walt ruled alcove one. He stood on his seat orating to the rapt attention of five or six bookish types. He was very unlike them in that he had a robust physique, thick dark wavy hair and an impressive moustache that reached all the way to the cheeks of his wide face. He was speaking especially loud to overcome the boos and the spitballs that were coming from alcove two.

"By allowing this, the university is saying yes to slaughtering dissidents in public squares, yes to conscripting ten-year-olds, yes to colluding with Hitler, yes to the mass murderer Mussolini!"

One of the minions, scribbling frantically in a notebook, stopped and raised his hand.

"What is it, Marcus?" Walt said. "I told you never to interrupt me!"

"I'm sorry," said Marcus. "But this pencil is too dull to take the minutes with, and I don't have a pencil sharpener."

"Oh, boy," Walt said with a roll of his eyes. "You'd show up at your own funeral unprepared!" He took a pencil sharpener from his front shirt pocket and tossed it Marcus' way. He failed to catch it. It bounced off the table, out of the alcove, and wound up not far from Bertram's feet. Marcus came over to pick it up. He looked up at Bertram and smiled, showing his terrible, rotting teeth.

Just as Bertram rose to move to a table farther away from those teeth, Lucinda Gold showed up. It was her that he had been waiting for. Attendant with the desire to live a satisfying life was the desire to live it with someone, and Lucinda was Bertram's girl. She didn't know it but she was the girl Bertram was going to ask to marry him.

Bertram was given much to flights of fancy, but lately he'd been having fantasies about bringing Lucinda home to meet Mother and Mother being jealous of her because she was beautiful and educated and young. He imagined them growing closer over the years, Mother won over by Lucinda's endearing qualities. He imagined the grandkids.

So he had made up his mind to do it. But he still hadn't decided when.

By this time the presence of Lucinda had precipitated a lull in the proceedings of the boys of alcove one. She was, simply put, a vision.

She took her surname very seriously in that her hair was quite literally the color of gold. Bertram could see where that would look a little dime-store on some women, but not on Lucinda. On her it looked sophisticated. On her it was a statement. Moreover, it wasn't even her greatest feature. She wore a sweater so form-fitting the threads were separating at the most strained points. Marcus leered in the most obvious way, exposing those obnoxious choppers.

"I have exactly nineteen minutes," she said to Bertram. Lucinda worked part-time in the Muni kitchen while she was attending the normal school just a few blocks away. She said she never imagined there was so much bookwork involved in becoming a teacher. Bertram helped her with the homework when he could, number one because she was his girl, but also because he thought she'd make a good teacher someday. He believed she was a person who had a lot to give.

They moved to another table and sat down to the lunch they had planned of sardines, apples and Postum, which Bertram carried around in a thermos.

He said, "That guy over there, he's setting the world on fire."

"That's Walter Escher," Lucinda said.

"You know him?"

"No, but I've had to listen to him all day. Alvin's in some classes with him." Alvin was Lucinda's brother, who also went to Muni. He wanted to be an architect someday, but Bertram was fond of saying he'd never go inside any building designed by Alvin Gold. He told Lucinda this Escher fellow was known among his classmates for being tough, sharp and completely intolerant of fools. Even his professors weren't spared. Escher had embarrassed some, shown up some, alienated others.

"He wants to abolish the ROTC on campus," said Lucinda.

"Why?"

"I don't know. Something about some Italian honor students visiting Muni. Something about the president of the university having breakfast with them."

"For someone who doesn't know, you know a lot," Bertram said.

"He's got this big poster with a drawing of soldiers marching with helmets on their heads, only the soldiers are all skeletons, and their faces are all gas masks. It's pretty scarifying."

"How do you know that?"

"He's got it taped to the wall of the alcove, Bertie," she said. "Sheesh."

Bertram hadn't noticed that. But then political business had a way of passing him by. Sometimes he actually admired guys like Walt not because they had all the answers but because they really thought they did. They believed in something. Bertram would have liked to feel that kind of passion, but it was such a strenuous effort. He wished it was more like the numbers that came so easily to him—neat, orderly, inevitable. Not so obscure. Not so mired in the fervent conceits of fervent men.

And speaking of Walt, wasn't Bertram the one who introduced Earl to him, and vice versa?

Was it fair of Earl to take take take all the time and not give back even something as simple as good news?

Bertram took up the letter opener that sat on the table with the pens and pencils in a black coffee mug with a broken-off handle. He slipped it under the edge of the seal of the envelope.

The opener made a clean, perfect cut.

Walt, of course, was right.

He slipped out the letter and unfolded it.

"Dear Mr. Castle,

It gives me great pleasure to inform you..."

5

"I don't know. Shouldn't we go to my office instead? What if someone comes in?"

Earl opened his eyes, breaking the crust that had formed at their corners. The first thing he thought was how unlike him it was to have a dream about school that didn't involve forgetting to study for a test or write a paper.

"We've been through this. This is the safest place to be. The trash baskets in the offices are emptied every night. There's no way we could all fit in your office anyway."

He remembered where he was now. He was not sure who the first voice belonged to, but the second he recognized immediately as Calvin's.

"And you think the janitors won't come in here? Where there are mops and pails and...

whatever that thing is over there?"

"It's a floor buffer, ma'am," came a deep voice noticeably inflected by Spanish.

"They only use this room for storage," Calvin said. "Now please, Sonia, relax."

Sonia? As in Rasmussen-Vell?

"And they're not janitors," came a different, much younger female voice. "They're custodial workers."

"That's right," added some soft-voiced male.

"I know. I'm sorry."

That was Rasmussen alright. She was forever sorry. For not having the syllabus until a month into the semester. For not having the papers graded by the time she promised. For actually not showing up for a class without telling anyone to put a sign up or anything. It had often seemed to Earl that she was indirectly apologizing for her acute inadequacy as an educator—for her very presence in front of the students—and in that sense she had much to be sorry for.

In fact, just being in the same room with her made Earl start to shake and sweat, but he suppressed any movement or sound.

"It's just that…what if somebody comes in?"

she said. "What would we do?"

"No one will come in!" Calvin barked. "My janitor buddy wouldn't steer me wrong. I mean, my custodial worker buddy."

"No," said the Spanish-inflected voice. "Janitor is okay. If you ask us what we do, that's what we say."

The young woman said, "That's a word invented to demean you and keep you down."

Even in his foggy state, Earl knew that wasn't true.

But something else was bothering him.

It was Calvin's buddy the janitor.

Earl was surprised to have felt a pang when he heard that. It was ridiculous—he'd never heard of the guy before. He had no indication that Calvin was getting it on with him.

But suddenly he was imagining the guy exactly where he was laying right now.

"It's respect for people like you that's part of why we're doing all this," the young woman went on, still not finding the tone she was seeking.

"That's right," said the unidentified male voice.

"If everybody doesn't keep it down," Calvin said, "we might not even make it through the first night."

A hush fell over the group.

Earl didn't know what was happening or what they were planning to do, but the mix of hope and urgency in Calvin's voice reminded him of the talk about "big changes" coming soon. About all that was clear to him at that moment was that they didn't know he was ten feet from them, hidden by the shelves, splayed on the stack of gym mats in exactly the position he had passed out. He sensed they were not likely to appreciate his presence there if they found out about it, so he just laid there and tried not to breathe audibly, which maybe was the best thing for him anyway, considering his hangover. In his life he had had three hangovers. The first was when he was a teenager, at a cousin's wedding. The second was during the year he entered Muni, in a strange bed after a night of drinking in the bars along Christopher Street. The one he had now was by far the worst.

In an unthinking instant, he turned his head slightly and his hair made a scraping sound against the mat.

"What was that?" Rasmussen said.

"You didn't hear anything," Calvin told her.

"I did. Oh God—are there rats in here?"

A laughter broke out among some of them. The younger woman said, "I knew it was a mistake bringing her in on this."

"Stay cool, Sonia!" Calvin said.

"I'm sorry. I just..." She started to cry.

"Here we go again," the young woman said.

"There are no rats in here, ma'am," said the accented man.

"I said all along that she doesn't have what it takes to be in on this."

Perhaps everyone expected Rasmussen to defend herself. All they got was wounded sniffling.

"That's not very nice, Isabel," said the soft male voice.

"The truth hardly ever is, Seth," Isabel said.

"Will you all please be quiet!" said Calvin. "If we're gonna get through this, if we're going to make it work, then we have to be united. You should be grateful Professor Rasmussen is with us, Isabel. It makes us stronger to have a member of the faculty on our side."

"That's right," said Seth.

"We have to remain together."

There was general agreement from the group.

Isabel sucked it up and said, "I'm sorry, professor."

"Please call me Sonia. And I'm sorry, too. It's just that the last twenty-four hours have been probably the worst day of my life."

"Shhhhhhhh!"

They went mute again. In the long moments that ensued, Earl heard sniffs and ticks and what he perceived to be a faint whistling in the air vent.

All the while a nauseous feeling made vague threats against his insides.

He took a deep, quiet breath and shut his eyes. He opened them again when Seth said, "Calvin, how long do you think we're gonna be here?"

"We've got about three minutes until the security guards change shift. Remember, everyone, we'll only have exactly ten minutes to do what we need to do before the cafeteria workers start coming in."

"But, I mean, how long do you think we're gonna be, you know, here."

In the sudden silence that followed Earl could easily imagine that suspicious stare Calvin sometimes employed. He said, "You're not questioning your commitment to the cause, are you buddy?"

"No…"

"Because there's no place for that here. There's no way we're gonna win this thing unless we all are totally committed. And besides, at this point, there's no going back."

"Well, that's not true," said Seth, laughing a little. "If someone wanted to leave now or any other time, they could."

"No one can leave now," Calvin said. "It's too late."

And Calvin left that uncomfortable feeling in the air.

Finally Isabel piped up: "Don't panic, Seth. We've all had to make other plans to go through with this. We've all had to arrange our lives so we could be gone for a while."

"I know," Seth said. "It's just my mother. She wakes up every morning about now. She's probably just finding out I'm not there…"

Earl was reminded of Bertram, just as everyone else was reminded of the people they had at home.

A walkie-talkie crackled to life. Earl couldn't

make it out at all, but Calvin spoke back to it.

"Go ahead."

"Kcikwekrkkz alipakkghilrtle alitcrick krawpzzmungklclat."

"Negative. We're sticking with the plan. The only way this is gonna work is if we stick with the plan."

"Krikjzakrekak,"

"Copy that."

Earl thought he sounded like a movie. Or maybe there was just something about walkie-talkies that made a person talk that way. In any case, he recalled again his old G.I. Joe.

More silence. Then Calvin explained that the security guard in the Kirsch Science Building was seen leaving a little early. The person on the other walkie-talkie, presumably someone inside Kirsch, wanted to go ahead and "start operations."

Perhaps there were some nods, but nobody said anything.

After a minute Calvin spoke again: "All I was saying, Seth, is that we're all in this together, right? This thing is more important than any one of us and any selfish personal concerns we might have, right?"

Earl thought that wasn't what Calvin had been saying at all, but Seth said, "Yeah I know."

"A lot of us are risking much more than you are. Look at Sonia. Look at Rogerio. They're risking their jobs."

"And that is incredibly brave," Seth observed.

Of course the only thing Rasmussen was risking at this point was a nervous breakdown, Earl thought. Obviously it was not public knowledge that she no longer had a job to lose.

Again the walkie-talkie startled Earl. Whatever was going on, the time had come to get it started.

Calvin said, "Copy that. Showtime, folks. Everyone knows what they're doing, right?"

A cautious shuffling was audible. Out of the corner of his eye Earl could see the EXIT sign dim, and they were gone.

He had to get out of there. But when he forced himself to sit up, he was quickly overcome by his nausea. He lurched toward an empty bucket and surrendered to the convulsions.

It was then Calvin poked his head from around the shelves.

"What the fuck? What the fuck? I thought I heard you back here! What the fuck!"

Earl just heaved.

"What? You're puking? Oh, man."

"…Calvin…"

"Damn! What the fuck are you still doing here?"

"I fell asleep, I guess."

"Fell asleep? You mean you passed out? I never met such a faggot-ass drinker as you!"

"Hey, fuck you!"

"Alright. Come on now. You gotta get up and get outta here!"

Earl went to stand up but as soon as he bent his knee he cried out and fell back to the mats.

"What the fuck are you doing?" Calvin said.

"Oh God! Oh God!"

"What's the matter?"

"My knee, Calvin, my knee…"

"What's wrong with it?"

"Oh fucking Jesus."

"Alright. Settle down a minute. I gotta get you outta here!"

"What the fuck do you guys think you're doing anyway?"

"We're taking over the damn school, what do you think?!"

"Taking it over? What does that mean?"

"It means exactly what I said."

"But why?"

"We've got reasons."

"Who's we? You and those other people? You and that idiot Rasmussen?"

"There's a lot more of us. Rasmussen was sort of a last-minute addition. After what you told me, I figured she had found out she was getting canned. So I went to her office and asked her to join us in the takeover." Calvin bit his lip. Then he spun around and put his hands on his head and said, "I gotta get you out of here!"

"How? You said there was no way out."

"Not without being seen…"

"Well I don't care if anyone sees me or not. I just want to get out of here and go home."

Calvin clasped his hands like he was praying and pressed them to his lips. He fell back a step. For seconds he was captured by thought. He stepped up again.

"I can't let you leave," he said.

"What? I'm leaving, Calvin."

"It's too risky right now."

"It's not too risky for me. I'm not involved with

this."

Calvin looked at his watch. "I know you're not," he said. "But it's already too late."

"Just help me up. I'll take it from there."

"You can't leave, Earl."

They looked at each other. Earl tried not to show any of the unease he was starting to feel.

"What I mean is," Calvin said, "the exits are all sealed by now."

Was this really Calvin, the eternal dawdler, acting with what appeared to be such purpose and determination? And had they really had this thing planned down to the minute? Had Earl read him all wrong?

He gripped his knee with both hands in an attempt to contain the pain.

"Damn."

Calvin knelt to him. "It's alright, Earl. I can get you out, but we have to wait for things to calm down a little."

"How long is that going to take?"

"I don't know."

Earl was beginning to think there was something seriously wrong with his leg. He had sudden, ridiculous visions of blood clots and amputations. He said, "I have to go to a hospital."

"It's not that bad. I'm going to take you somewhere where you can lie down awhile. Put your arm around my neck. You ready?"

Earl felt weightless when Calvin picked him up.

Calvin carried him out of the maintenance room and whisked him through the corridors. Earl had never seen them so empty before. They looked bigger, almost cavernous. The glass wall that overlooked the campus had been completely covered by large sheets of heavy brown paper. The dim light from the embedded ceiling fixtures made everything look a little misty. The darkened classrooms roared with empty air as they flew past.

Earl had an odd sensation of being in the presence of something hallowed.

They arrived at the freight elevator. With an elbow and a foot, Calvin parted its doors and the iron grating inside, careful all the while not to drop Earl or bump his knee. In the same way, he closed the doors. He dug into the set of keys that hung from a belt loop, finding the one that started the elevator.

They rode up one floor and Calvin went through the whole process in reverse.

The glass wall on this floor, Earl saw, had been papered over as well.

In no time Calvin had his office door open and Earl inside.

He placed Earl gently in his chair, then shut the door and turned on the light.

The office looked completely different than when Earl was there hours before. It had been set up as some kind of command center. Calvin's desk had been cleared of its usual clutter to make way for a portable black-and-white TV, its antenna cocked forward, and a small radio. They were both on but with their volumes turned so low they could scarcely be heard. On the wall was a map of the Muni campus, which Earl recognized as the same one on the inside cover of this semester's course catalog. It was marked at various points by red pushpins. In the corner was a large styrofoam cooler, its cover unable to completely close.

Calvin pulled a sleeping bag from under his desk and rolled it open on the floor.

He picked Earl up and laid him gently on the sleeping bag.

Without asking he carefully rolled up his pant leg so he could have a look at the knee.

"Do you know anything about injuries?" Earl said.

"I know that definitely looks swollen. Does it still hurt?"

It did, but somehow, with Calvin tending to it, it wasn't so bad. Calvin went over to the cooler, opened it, and plunged his hand into the ice. He pulled out a bottle of beer and handed it to Earl.

"No thanks. I'm still recovering from last night."

"It's for your knee, stupid. Hold it against your knee. Like this."

Earl did so but the cold bottle was wet and shocking and it slipped from his hand and hit the floor rolling, alarming Calvin until he saw that it didn't break.

"Try to be careful," he said, picking it up and handing it to him again.

"It's my problem holding booze."

Calvin laughed a little. Earl wanted to see if he could still make him laugh.

Calvin opened the top drawer of his desk and found a small bottle of aspirin. He shook out a few into Earl's hand.

"I have to leave you here now," he said. "But I'll be back. So just stay put, alright?"

"Where are you going?"

"I have to see to some things."

"When will you be back?"

"Soon."

"I hope so."

"I'll bring you back something to eat."

Earl realized that he was hungry.

"You look tired too. So you just relax here and nap a little and stay off that knee, right?"

"Right. No jumping jacks."

As soon as Calvin was gone, Earl thought about leaving. He thought about dragging himself to the nearest supposedly sealed exit and then hobbling his way down the hill to the subway station.

But his knee was still not cooperating. Moreover, his insides ached from the vomiting and he still had a hangover. The temptation to do what Calvin told him to do—to simply lay his head on the pillow and go to sleep—was strong.

Then again, how could he sleep at a time like this?

He looked around the office.

Calvin's phone had been left on the floor to make way for the TV and radio. Earl reached and dragged it by its cord toward him.

He grabbed the receiver. A weird beeping emanated from it. A sticker next to the numbers instructed him to dial 97 to get an outside line. He did, and then dialed the only number he could think of.

The line rang once before Bertram picked it up.

"Hello?"

"Hi. It's me."

"Earl? Earl? Are you alright?"

"Yes."

"Where are you?"

And suddenly he realized that calling Bertram was a mistake. He had reached out, he supposed, because he knew Bertram cared about him and his well-being and he wanted to let the old man know that he was okay. But he had essentially done that in the first few seconds of the call, and now there was nothing left to say.

"I just wanted to…call."

"Well that's thoughtful of you, Earl, even though it is five o'clock in the morning. Where are you?"

Earl did not respond.

"Are you sure you're alright?"

"Yes, I'm alright."

"Then why do you sound so strange?"

"I don't sound strange."

"You don't?"

"No."

"Okay. So where are you?"

"That's not important."

"It's not?"

"No."

"Okay. Well I'm glad you're calling, Earl, but the better thing to do would have been to call last night. I was worried."

Again Earl went silent.

"I mean, I was just concerned that maybe something had happened to you, that's all. Who you spend the night with is your business, of course. You're an adult and you can come and go as you please. I know you would never let anything interfere with your studies. Earl? Are you there?"

"Yes."

"Is there anything else you want to tell me,

Earl?"

"Just…don't worry."

That was something Bertram could not say "okay" to. "Are you coming home soon?"

"I'm not sure. But I really should get off the phone now."

"Okay." Bertram was looking at the letter that he had put back atop the frosted vessel. "I'll see you soon, I hope. Let me know if there's anything I can do to help, okay?"

"Okay," Earl said. "Bye."

"Bye, Earl."

Earl hung up and gently laid himself back on the sleeping bag.

As he started to drift off, he began to think that maybe Calvin was making too much of this whole takeover business. It could very simply blow over, perhaps even by the end of the day.

Daniel Scott

6

Bertram stepped into his slippers and made his way to the kitchen.

He poured a mug's worth of water into the coffeemaker and a scoop of coffee into its basket and stood watching as it dripped and hissed.

He poured the brew into the mug and added a dollop of heavy cream.

He took it to the living room and sipped it in the padded reclining chair that Jo had always said was too big for the apartment, but which Bertram insisted upon.

"It's a hard life without a comfortable chair," he had told her.

Nearly two hours had passed since Earl's call. Bertram never fell back to sleep.

Again, the apartment was much calmer than

usual with no Earl running around.

On a normal day, Earl would be toasting a slice of white bread, eating it with nothing on top, and washing it down with black coffee, all the while buried in some book or xeroxed article or reciting facts memorized for an exam that day.

Sometimes his preoccupations were less obvious.

But though Bertram was always the first to say "Good morning," Earl never failed to say "Good morning" back.

He reclined slightly as his eyes drifted across the room, past the oak china cabinet—itself an insistence of Jo's—then over the bookcase, its shelves filled with volumes undusted since Jo's passing and unread for many more years than that. They took up valuable space in the place, but Bertram never forgot the English professor he had at Muni who told the class that throwing away a book was "a treason of humanity—yours and everyone else's."

Perhaps this professor had lived in a spacious suburb. And he had, as Bertram recalled, been declared by Walt to be "one of the very, very many dullards who were employed by The

Municipal University." He said the pay there was low so the good ones went elsewhere. That at least was what Lucinda Gold was told by her brother Alvin, who was paraphrasing Walt. It bespoke a withering arrogance about Walt that it was not at all nice to be on the receiving end of, as Bertram himself found out not long after learning who Walt was.

It was exactly one week after that memorable day in the cafeteria that Bertram showed up there again for a quick bite with Lucinda. All day he had had trouble paying attention in class. All day he had been feeling the hard lump in his pants— the box that held the ring that he was going to give to Lucinda. He had had to use all his savings on the down payment, even despite the jeweler being his mother's cousin. When he imagined it, it all came together quite easily: his question, her response, their happiness. But the reality was much tougher.

But as usual she was late, and Bertram found himself listening again to Walter Escher. Only this time Walt's smart clothes were smeared with what at first looked like blood. His followers were in similar shape. But as Bertram saw on closer inspection, none of them have been bloodied at all. They'd been splattered. With tomatoes and eggs and God knows what else. Bertram almost laughed, not to spite them but just because they looked so ridiculous, and Walt the most ridiculous of all. The guy could have cleaned himself up a little, but he didn't. He had some piece of garbage on his shoulder. All it would take was a little flick of the finger to get rid of it. But he wanted it there, for dramatic effect.

He pounded the table. "We will not be deterred by thugs or the brutality of the New York City police force..."

He stopped all of a sudden. Bertram felt Walt's eyes trace an outline around him, then fit him into it. Then the whole lot of them turned and looked at Bertram.

"You there," Walt said. "Do we know you?"

"No, I..."

"You were hanging around here yesterday, weren't you?"

"No, I..."

"You're one of Stuckey's people, aren't you?"

"I told you," Marcus said.

What on Earth was a Stuckey, Bertram

wondered.

"You can report to Stuckey that we're assembling in accordance with our constitutional rights. And we'll protest when and where we deem appropriate. He needn't send spies around pretending to be fellow travelers. This isn't Soviet Russia."

"But I…"

"Run along, boy. Go."

"But I'm not…"

"How forcefully do you need the point to be made, my friend?"

So Bertram turned and walked away just because that was what he had wanted to do from the second Walt spotted him. He decided to wait for Lucinda in the lobby, where there was a line of phone booths—nice wooden ones, real roomy. He sat in one and started reading a book of poems by Delmore Schwartz as he waited. And wait he did. That girl knew no concept of time.

In the meantime he was approached by a strapping fellow who had put some kind of pomade in his hair.

"You," he said, "are you a friend of that guy in there?"

"What? What guy?"

"The bigmouth standing on his chair. The one I saw you talking with."

"It was more that he was talking to me."

"You want some advice? Stay away from him."

"What's the matter with him?"

"The matter with him is that he's trying to stir up people against their own country."

"How so?"

"He tried to disrupt the ROTC review today. Him and his little pals there. They practically started a riot. They're rowdies."

"Those guys?"

"Yup. But we were ready for them." He chuckled a bit. "We got them good."

"But aren't those guys just doing what they think is right?"

"Look," the guy said, "all I'm trying to do is help you out. For your own sake. Just stay away from them. My uncle works in the President's office so believe me when I say the university is running out of patience with them. They're the same guys that marched to President Hollis' house and practically knocked him to the ground when he came outside. Did you hear about that?"

He hadn't. But he was starting to wonder how he ever got entangled in any of this when, really, he wasn't involved in any way.

Lucinda, again, was his savior, showing up like she did. She had come out of the cafeteria. She stopped and looked at the both of them. The guy said, "I'll see you in class," even though he wasn't in any of Bertram's current courses, and he left.

"Lucinda, why are you coming from inside the cafeteria?"

"What are you doing out here?" she said. "Don't I get a kiss?"

He happily obliged.

"What were you talking to Rob Stuckey about?"

"Was that Stuckey? You know him?"

"Everybody knows him, Bertie. He's captain of the Muni track team. He's had his picture in the paper."

As it turned out, Walt would soon be the one with his picture in the paper. The protest was news. Even covered in swill, Walt took a handsome picture.

That was a fact Bertram knew would remain true about Walt for a lifetime; he had several of

Walt's books, each with a smiling full-page picture in the back.

He wanted to get Walt to sign them one day, but he kept forgetting to ask.

He turned his attention from the bookcase to the solid oak desk that faced it. It had been Bertram's ever since his mother died half a century ago. A small lamp sat atop it, turned on.

He had left it on when he went to bed so Earl would not have to stumble in in the dark.

It made him a little angry, this thoughtful gesture of his going unappreciated by Earl, like so many thoughtful gestures had in the past. Earl could have called last night. He could have let him know he wasn't coming home. The wasted electricity from the lamp being on wouldn't come out of Earl's pocket—just another of Bertram's thoughtful little gestures.

Of course the cost to run the lamp was negligible, and it was a thoughtful gesture on Earl's part that it was even there in the first place. He had won a hundred-dollar award from the school for an essay he'd written. That evening he brought the lamp home. The lamp itself was really nothing, just a black ceramic base and a black lampshade—only Earl would buy a lamp with a black shade—but Bertram was so touched by the unexpected contribution to the household, he almost came to tears.

"That's awfully nice of you, Earl," he had said solemnly.

The young man shrugged. "It's always too dark in this apartment anyway."

"But you won that money. You should have spent it on something for yourself," Bertram said, even though Earl had, in a way, done just that, and he only spent a fraction of the prize.

Still, whenever Bertram looked at the lamp, he came to the conclusion that Earl wasn't really a bad kid. Cantankerous at times, yes. Self-involved, unquestionably. But he didn't waste his time and energy like so many his age did.

And Bertram always said a person had to make allowances for Earl because, after all, he was raised by brutes—Jo herself had called them that, much to Bertram's amusement.

Earl's grandmother always harbored a deep distaste for the family she helped create.

In her lowest moments, she shook her head and said she was assured of a place in hell for never quite masking her resentment toward the existence of her children Colleen (Earl's mother) and Vaughn (Earl's uncle). They were reminders of when she was not as aware of the things she was doing as she became after meeting Bertram.

"You're too hard on yourself, my dear," Bertram had told her. "You fed them. You clothed them. You did all the things a mother is supposed to do."

"Not all of them," she said.

"What more is there?"

"I was supposed...to love them."

"Oh, well, my sweet, you can't blame yourself for something you have no control over."

Water began to rise in Jo's green eyes.

"Besides," he said, touching her face, "there's no such place as hell anyway."

At first, Bertram always believed Jo was exaggerating about her family. He considered it a common affliction among gentiles nowadays to think their families were worse than everybody else's. He blamed it on Phil Donahue and Oprah Winfrey and all the other lurid talk shows that had become the rage lately.

But then he actually met Jo's family.

It was at one of the big summer barbecues Colleen had every year. Bertram and Jo stayed side by side in lawn chairs that would not sit flatly on the pebbly ground of Colleen's backyard.

Colleen, Vaughn and Vaughn's wife Stephanie sat across a long table cloaked in a blue flower cloth.

Vaughn and Stephanie's kids were splashing in the aboveground pool.

Bees kept swooping in front of people's faces and hovering over the food. Colleen seemed unfazed by them, but then she brought out the bug spray. She shot it into the air overhead. Bertram watched as the poison mist settled over everything on the table.

Colleen had not seen much of her mother since Jo impulsively sold the house in Crompaugue and absconded to Manhattan with the money and this man she'd met on a walking tour called "The Bridges and Waterways of Central Park"—the same man who was now not eating the grilled chicken or the red-skinned potato salad on the compartmented plastic plate in front of him.

Jo had failed to disclose to Colleen what she got for the house. Colleen was forced to just come right out and ask. Jo said she didn't pry into Colleen's finances and that she should be afforded the same courtesy.

"I wasn't prying, Mother. I just don't know why it's such a big secret."

"There's no big secret," Jo said.

"I'll bet Bertram knows."

Again, whether he did or he didn't was none of her business.

Bertram, who had made sure his cowlick wasn't sticking up and devoured breath mints on the drive from the city, found himself with very little to say. He was starting to think he should have listened when Jo said she didn't want to go to the barbecue. But he had claimed it was too strange for him not to meet the family of the woman he took to the justice of the peace. She finally confessed her fear that once he met them he wouldn't love her anymore. He said that was nonsense.

At one point, Bertram asked where the bathroom was and when it became clear Colleen had no intention of answering Jo had to say, "It's the second door when you go in, honey."

He found the toilet seat and the tank wrapped

in a furry blue covering that looked newly bought. The toilet paper was almost a paler blue than the blue of the drawn window shade. He washed his hands with the blue-colored soap and got out of there.

He was probably right to think this was the only time he'd ever be alone in Colleen Castle's house—maybe even the only time ever—so he gave in to his curiosity and had a look around.

Bertram had lived in New York apartments all his life. They were invariably too small, but Bertram had never been in one that didn't look crammed with life. You could get to know a person just by looking around.

Whenever he visited homes in the suburbs, however, he came away thinking they were too big and too empty, with too many places to hide things away.

He passed the kitchen, stopping long enough to take in the spotless appliances. There was an icemaker in the door of the refrigerator. The small window above the sink was decorated with frilly yellow curtains. On the sill sat a large glass knickknack of some kind. On closer inspection Bertram determined it was a representation of a wishing well.

The next room was where the TV was. A coffee table with a tinted glass top stretched out in front of a leathery sofa the simple size of which would prevent it from ever getting past Bertram's front door. Glass objects were placed around the room, wherever there was a surface for one.

The next room had an expensive-looking all-black stereo system. Massive speakers, each the height of a small child, sat on either side of the main component, which had far too many knobs and switches for Bertram to ever bother with. Beneath it was a shelf full of albums. Here also was a small table entirely devoted to the glass objects.

He was about to move on when he noticed the adolescent Earl sitting in a chair at a window that looked out to the street, his elbows propped on the sill. He had been nowhere to be found at the barbecue, nor had any mention of him been made.

Bertram moved closer. Earl was pressing against the screen window, holding back just enough so the screen wouldn't give.

Earl turned to look at the old man. The skin on his forehead retained the impression of the screen.

The rest of his face was wet from crying.

"What's wrong, kid?" Bertram said.

Earl wiped his nose on his sleeve, shuddered, and said, "I hate this."

"Hate what?"

"This."

"You mean everything?"

"No. Just this."

"This isn't gonna last forever," Bertram said. He pulled out a handkerchief and handed it to the boy. "I'm Bertram."

"I know who you are," he said, taking the handkerchief and wiping his face.

"You do?"

"The guy who eloped with my grandmother."

"You know all about me."

"My mother's done nothing but complain about you all day."

"No kidding?"

"She doesn't like you." He wiped his face dry. "I think it's because you're Jewish."

Bertram detected no malice in that remark. It was merely clear-eyed in the innocent way of youth.

"And what about you?" Bertram said.

"What about me?"

"Do you hate me because I'm Jewish?"

"I didn't say she hated you. I said she doesn't like you. She's afraid you'll take all of Grandma's money. Me, I don't even really know what Jewish means."

"A lot of Jews wonder about that same thing."

"All religions are equally stupid anyway," Earl announced.

"They are?"

"I don't even believe in God."

"Why not?"

"I think the question is 'Why?' If someone came up to you and said, 'Oh, by the way, there's this big invisible being who knows everything and sees everything and decides when you die and whether you go to paradise or suffer an eternity of torture,' you wouldn't say 'Why not?' You'd say 'Why?'" He pulled back a little, as if he was reconsidering the merits of his argument.

That was the first time—there were to be many more—that Earl reminded him of an old friend he had, Walt. The surety. The foundation in logic. The fearlessness. Even with a tear-stained face and a snotty nose.

They seemed to realize at the same time that Colleen was watching them from the doorway. She had in her hands a package of hot dog buns just retrieved from the kitchen.

"I thought you might have drowned," she said to Bertram, sounding a little disappointed.

"No," Bertram said. "I'm still here."

"Earl, why don't you come out and say hello to your cousins?"

Earl didn't respond, but turned back to the window overlooking the street.

Bertram turned to leave. On his way out, he said to her, "He's alright. Just the teenage blues." She shot him a look that said it was none of his business. And it was true, Bertram thought. You can't tell people how to raise their own kids. He would feel the same way, were he in that position.

He left, but halted just outside the screen door. He had stopped to get a view of the shaped shrubs in the front yard, but he heard the conversation continuing inside.

Colleen's words took on a lashing quality.

"What the hell is wrong with you? You mope around, you don't talk to anybody, you act like nothing's good enough for you. I'm sick of you.

And now I come in here and find you bawling your eyes out to that…that decrepit old Jew!"

Earl made no reply that Bertram could hear.

"And what's all this nonsense about you not believing in God anymore? It's bad enough you turn your back on your own family, but now God's not good enough for you? I thank God your father's not alive to hear his son talking like this. You've damned yourself, Earl. You're damned and you better realize it."

Bertram couldn't stand to hear any more. He returned to his place next to Jo and did not utter one word the rest of the time.

On the drive back to the city, Bertram told Jo about his encounter with Earl. She dropped her head into her hands. Her bad feeling about her family extended to every member of it.

"There's no explaining them," she said. "There's only apologizing for them."

But Bertram said he rather liked the kid, calling him "uncommonly intelligent," a fact that had somehow gone lost on Jo and Colleen and apparently everyone the boy had ever encountered in the dim insularity of Crompaugue. Earl himself seemed not entirely cognizant of it.

After the cookout, Jo and Colleen simply stopped seeing each other. Instead there were terse phone calls that usually left Jo in a foul mood. Bertram said he felt bad about coming between her and her family.

Earl was virtually a grownup the next time Bertram saw him, at Jo's funeral.

He hardly looked to Bertram like that confused boy of five years before. There was something hard in his countenance now; his was a face that would never allow itself to be so easily rent by emotions as it once was.

But Earl was the only member of his family who even bothered to talk to Bertram, who was sobbing relentlessly. Bertram couldn't have known it was mostly just to spite his mother that Earl stepped up and offered his handkerchief the way Bertram once had offered his to him.

"Thank you, Earl," he said.

"You remembered my name," Earl said.

In the corner of his vision, Earl saw his mother in a disapproving stance.

He took one of the black funeral home chairs and set it down next to Bertram. They had straight backs and short seats and were impossible to slouch in.

"Your mother," Bertram said, "she's not so fond of me."

"The best thing to do is act like she doesn't exist."

"That's not going to be easy."

"Why?"

"Because she still doesn't know what your grandmother's will says."

"Oh, right. The money."

"That's been the reason she's hated me all this time. You told me that, Earl. Remember?"

Earl adopted a searching look.

Although five years at Earl's age might in some cases just as well be a hundred, Bertram was quite sure he did remember.

"You were kind of upset that day," Bertram said, but he quickly saw that he had embarrassed the young man. "It's okay. I took it as a sign of intelligence."

Earl laughed a little. He was glad, at least, that he had gotten the old man talking so that maybe he could think of something other than that the person he loved was gone forever.

"A thing I don't understand..." Bertram said,

blowing his nose, "...the people here—your mother—you, even..."

"What?"

"Nobody's crying. Nobody's sad."

"It's just not their way."

"Didn't they care about Jo?" That was a question he posed face to face, and Earl knew what he was really asking. For the first time, he felt ashamed of his lack of feeling.

"I don't know about them," he said. "But as for me, I really hadn't seen her in a long time. After she married you, she never came around."

Bertram nodded. "I'm sorry," he said. "I never meant to keep you away from your grandmother. I begged her to go see her family, even if she did it without me."

"I know she didn't like to come see us. I don't blame her. And I don't blame you."

He looked over at his mother. She was still keeping an eye on him. She turned full face to him, put up one hand and waved for him to come over. Earl turned away like he didn't see her.

"How come there's no one here from your side of the family?" he said to Bertram.

"There's no one left from my side of the

family."

"Don't you have any kids?"

"Once, a long time ago, I had a son. He was born sick and died as a little boy. Jerome Alan Berg. Center of the universe to nonexistent, just like that. Gloria, my first wife, had two miscarriages before she had him." He stopped because his voice broke up.

Earl said, "I'm sorry." He had recently learned that was the thing to say when people told you about bad things that had happened to them.

"Earl, listen to me. I'm going to tell you what Jo's will says."

"I hope she totally stiffed Colleen," said Earl, jumping at the chance to lighten the mood.

"You shouldn't call your mother by her first name. Colleen has nothing to worry about. The money's all hers."

"Damn."

"Most of it, anyway."

"Well, it's only right she left you something."

"She didn't leave me anything, Earl. I never wanted or needed Jo's money. But she left a small amount to you so you can go to college."

For a long moment Earl was silent.

"I wonder why she did that," he said.

"Because she believed you're smart enough to make something of yourself one day."

"Grandma believed that?"

"Sure."

A moment of silence passed between them. Bertram hemmed a little. "I mean, I suggested that she do that."

"You did?"

"When we talked that time at your mother's barbecue, you reminded me of someone I know. Someone who is brilliant."

"Who?"

"Someone I knew a long time ago. You'll understand when you're old like me. The point is, he was brilliant then and so are you now. I told your grandmother that."

"And what did she say?"

"Frankly, she didn't buy it."

Earl snorted like he shouldn't have even bothered to ask.

"But I told her she was wrong."

"And what makes you so sure that you're right?"

"Because even as a boy you saw right through

everything, even God, even your own mother. Plus, you had the heart to cry about it."

Earl became irritated. He didn't like the feeling of having been examined when he wasn't aware of it.

"And what if I don't want to go to college? How much money are we talking about here?"

"The stipulation is there's money only if you use it to go to school."

"Did you suggest that, too?"

The subject was dropped when they looked up and saw Colleen standing there. She had a sad smile on her face as she bent down to Bertram to say, "Bertram, I'm sorry about losing my mother, and I know you're sorry about losing your wife. I just want you to know that if you need anything, all you have to do is call."

She brought her face close to his and brushed her cheek against his very briefly. Then she turned and walked away.

"What was that all about?" Earl said.

Bertram smiled. "Your mother has her nice side too, right?"

He thought it best not to tell Earl what he was looking at that very minute: Colleen with Jo's lawyer, who had come to pay his respects. Colleen had learned the money was hers. That was the reason she came over. But Bertram was distressed at Earl's dislike of his mother—it did not seem natural—and he wanted him to think that she was capable of at least a little decency.

After the funeral, Bertram went back to life as a bachelor.

He had plenty of pictures of Jo, but packed away every last one. He could not, for the time being, bear to look at them. He would have been breaking up all day long.

On a Sunday morning a few weeks later, Earl called. He was in the city. He wanted to know if he could stop by and talk.

"Absolutely, Earl," Bertram said. "Come right over."

Bertram dressed and tidied the place somewhat, not that it needed it. He was more than a little excited about Earl's visit. It had been a long while since anyone besides himself crossed the threshold of his door. Indeed, when the buzzer went off, he was startled until he remembered what it was.

Earl looked terrible. Unshaven. Hair a mess.

Clothes like he slept in them. "Earl," Bertram said, "you look like you spent the night walking the streets."

"Can I come in?"

"Absolutely. Why don't I make us both a nice breakfast?"

"It's up to you," Earl said, which Bertram took to mean yes.

Coffee brought Earl more to life, and made him more willing to answer questions from Bertram as he fried eggs and toasted English muffins.

"How's your mother?"

"Same."

"And your uncle?"

"Beats me."

"And you, Earl? How are you?"

Bertram saw in him the same confused teenager from years ago. He was glad Earl had not changed that much after all.

But this time Earl did not cry. He took a short break in the inhalation of his food. "I wanna go to college," he said.

"Great! What do you want to study?"

"I don't know."

"Where do you want to go?"

"I have no idea. I only know it can't be in Crompaugue. I can't stand that place anymore."

"Well, hating your hometown is not the best reason to go to college, Earl. Though it is a pretty common one."

Bertram sensed there was something, probably several things, that Earl wasn't telling him, something that led him to show up out of the blue looking so haggard and desperate to change the direction of his life. But he didn't press.

"Did you go to college?" Earl said.

"Yes I did. Municipal University."

"That's still around, isn't it?"

"Yes it is. It's changed a lot since I was there…"

"The thing is"—and here's where the tears started—"I don't know how to do it."

"Do what, Earl?"

"Go to college. I mean, I don't know how to go about it."

And Bertram, who had known what he had to do to go to college as early as the first grade and had heard no end of his parents' expectations for him, saw what Earl was struggling against, how the boy had been forced to dull his natural intelligence as a way of not enraging the people around him. It left him hobbled by sadness and doubt.

"The first thing you have to do is call the college and get them to send you an application," Bertram said.

"Okay. So I just fill out the application and send it in?"

"There's a little more to it than that. Don't worry. I'll walk you through it."

"Thank you," Earl said. At the time Bertram did not realize how rare those words were coming from Earl Castle.

Bertram put his coffee on the side table and picked up the TV remote. He flipped around until he came to something that looked distantly familiar—not the modern glass-and-concrete building in the foreground, but the one behind it with the Gothic spires. In Bertram's time it was known as Gunther Hall and he attended classes in it.

The station was a just-started cable channel focused solely on New York City news.

The camera pulled back to show a large crowd of people milling around the red-brick plaza.

There were young folks with book bags strapped to their backs. There were cops in uniform. A man with a bullhorn standing higher than the rest accentuated whatever he was saying with pumps of his fist. There were TV news vans.

Then he thought to read the words on the lower part of the screen. He took out his glasses.

STUDENTS SEIZE BUILDINGS AT MUNICIPAL U.

Bertram nearly fell out of his chair as he scrambled to the phone and dialed. "Turn on the news!" he said.

"I have it on," Walt said. "It's pretty impressive, huh?"

"What?"

"I have to admit I didn't think the kids today had it in them. This is just like the old days!"

"What?"

"Actually, this is more than we ever really did. I mean, we never actually shut down the college!"

"Earl's in there!"

"What?"

"I know, I can't believe it either!"

"Wow. Well, good for him."

"What?"

"It shows he's thinking of something bigger than himself. I have to admit that sometimes that boy is a little scary."

Walt would never forget his first meaningful encounter with Earl. Walt had come over and Bertram was running late. Earl had answered the door holding *State and Revolution*, one of the more famous of Lenin's many treatises. Walt always had a soft spot for Lenin, and it is one that he retained, despite the worldwide discrediting of his hero that was currently going on.

"Hey! You're reading old Vladimir Ilyich!" Few things brightened Walt's demeanor like the romance of his old heroes.

"It's for a class," Earl said. He didn't want Walt to think he was driven to it out of some kind of newfound revolutionary fervor.

"Good stuff, huh?"

Earl shrugged.

"You don't think so?"

Okay, if he really wanted to talk about it, he would.

"Reads like raving."

"Really?"

"His chief concern is showing how he, and

only he, is the one who truly understands Marx."

"He took his role as an interpreter of one of the great thinkers very seriously."

"No, he is all about consolidating his own power. He casts himself in the role of the purest oracle, but behind it he is scheming to discredit his rivals. Those he accuses most viciously of incorrectly interpreting Marx are those he perceives as the greatest threat."

"I think that's very cynical, Earl. I think Lenin really believed in the ideas of Marx. He believed in the rightness of Marx's analysis of class structures."

"I don't say he didn't really believe in Marx. But he may have had, in his most honest private moments, his doubts about the applicability of his analysis to the real world, to real human nature."

"That depends on what you believe human nature to be, Earl. Apparently you believe human nature is to be selfish and scheming. But I believe it to be compassionate and concerned for the welfare of others. I have to believe that's the case. If I didn't believe that, if I believed what you do, I think I would have killed myself a long time ago."

"You have no idea what I believe. All you

know is a few observations I've made about Lenin and *State and Revolution*. Please don't presume that you've somehow read my entire psyche, because if you really had you'd know that my own personal true feelings lie somewhere much closer to your own. Just because I don't agree with you about Lenin's intentions, just because my late twentieth-century perspective allows me to see him as the founder of a system of oppression responsible for the deaths of millions of people, does not make me some kind of monster. As for Marx, I agree his analysis of the class inequities is brilliant, but his relationship to the Marxists is a lot like that of Jesus' to the Christians: far less noble-minded people have appropriated the words of a great man and used them to commit all sorts of atrocities."

Earl went into his room then, leaving Walt to wait for Bertram alone. Walt had learned that Earl was someone to be reckoned with. But Walt saw too that he was almost reckless in the sure use of his intellect, perhaps to the point of sabotaging himself.

"He's ruining everything right now!" Bertram said. "No valedictorian, no Rhyman scholarship.

He'll be just another bum with a degree from Muni! And that's only if they let him graduate."

"Some things are more important than awards and accolades, Bert."

"That's fine for you to say, Walt, but this may be the only chance Earl has. You know his background, where he came from…"

They fell silent as a reporter began speaking urgently. Bertram could hear her on his television as well as on Walt's, through the phone:

…police and university officials have confirmed that four of the buildings on the Muni campus have been taken over by student protesters…

…the protesters are demanding that the recently announced tuition hikes be repealed, and that there be no faculty or staff layoffs and no cuts in financial aid…

…a spokesman for Muni, Mark Redecki, says the school understands that these budget decisions are painful, but he says they're necessary given the gloomy fiscal outlook for the city and the state…

…the takeover of these buildings is not an acceptable way of airing grievances, and

that all involved students have been immediately suspended and face permanent expulsion...

"Oh no," Bertram said.

"Take it easy, Bert."

"That's it. It's over. Expelled students don't get Rhyman scholarships."

"The school is just making threats at this point. I don't even know how many times I got threatened with expulsion. I'll bet they don't even know the names of the students inside the buildings."

"How could Earl do something so reckless like this?"

"Bert…"

"I'd better get off the line. He could be trying to call again."

He had to wonder how many people had ever hung up on Walt Escher in the middle of his saying something.

He breathed loudly through his nose as he stared at the television. The talking heads were moving on, promising to return to Muni for regular updates.

Bertram got up from his chair and sat at the

desk. The black lampshade let through a dark cast that almost made the spots on the back of his hands invisible.

He vowed the lamp would stay on until Earl came home.

Daniel Scott

7

Bertram and Walt were not the only ones watching the news at that moment. Earl sat rapt on the sleeping bag, his back to the wall, his recovering knee drawn up to his chin.

...school officials say they are in contact with the protesters...

Calvin had yet to return. Earl was starting to wonder if he ever would. First Rasmussen, now Calvin. Was there something about him that made people think it was okay to stand him up?

...hundreds of students are gathered outside the Fripp Academic Center, many of them signing petitions and chanting in support of the takeover...

Earl had thought about leaving. He even hobbled to the door, inched it open, and poked his head out. The corridor seemed to echo its own emptiness. From somewhere a current of air rushed past, cooling his face and slightly lifting a few of the flyers attached to the bulletin board.

At the near end of the hallway, the double doors leading to the stairwell had been rendered unusable by a chain looped again and again around the metal bars that opened them. It sagged in the middle with the weight of a gold-colored padlock.

The doors at the far end weren't even visible. They were, amazingly, barricaded by a ten-foot-high stack of silver metal chairs with padded black seats—the kind of chair found in every office of Muni. They weren't stacked neatly, but every which way, interlocking in an impossible design. It was a creation more of passion than sense, but it certainly got the job done.

The only exit from the corridor was the freight elevator, for which Calvin had the key. So, for the time being at least, Earl simply could not leave.

...the mayor has refused to step in, calling on the school and the protesters to work it out themselves.

The NYPD is here, but so far they're just

milling around, making sure the students gathered outside stay calm and orderly...

After the news, Earl turned the volume down and dozed again. He woke up immediately at the sound of keys at the door. Calvin came in at last. One of his shirttails was untucked. His glasses—which Earl had hardly ever seen him wear—sat crookedly on his face. His eyes were puffy and they looked surprised—shocked, even—when he laid them on Earl. Apparently he had forgotten all about him, which did not make Earl feel good. Then Calvin made a foul expression. "Ewww!" he said. "It fucking smells like piss in here!"

Earl had been there awhile. He had filled three empty beer bottles and was working on a fourth.

"What the hell was I supposed to do?" said Earl.

Calvin carefully picked up the bottles and took them out of the office, returning a moment later. He pulled a can of air freshener from one of the cabinets and sprayed it around. Earl felt the wet droplets burn across his face and arms.

Calvin took a short gold key off his key ring hooked to his belt buckle and snapped it down on the desk. "There's a janitor's closet next to the freight elevator. There's only a basin there, but it serves the purpose."

"It would have been nice if you'd left this before you disappeared for seven hours," said Earl, slipping the key into his shirt pocket.

"Things got a little crazy. I lost track of time. I assumed you'd be sleeping all this time."

Jesus, Earl thought. He couldn't pick just one excuse and stick with that?

"You said you would bring me something to eat."

"Oh shit!" Calvin said.

"I'm starving, Calvin!"

"Okay, okay." Earl watched as Calvin hopped up on his desk and reached upward. He pushed in the ceiling tile and slid it aside. He reached in and pulled out a bag of chips, tossing it down to Earl. Next came a can of peaches, a can of baked beans, a can opener.

"Wow," Earl said, tearing into the chips. "You really are prepared."

"Yeah, well, now that you know about my secret stash, don't clean me out." He hopped down.

"Nothing to drink?"

"Just beer. If you think you can handle it."

Earl refused. But then the chips made him thirsty, so he asked for one. He was surprised to find it tasted almost like nothing.

Calvin collapsed onto the sleeping bag. Earl sat upright at his feet, munching.

Calvin closed his eyes long enough for Earl to wonder if he had gone to sleep. But he opened them, looked at the TV, and said, "You've been watching the news."

"Yeah. Wow. Four buildings. How many people are involved in this thing?"

"Hundreds," Calvin said, tucking his hands behind his head.

"The news said that, but then they said the actual number was much lower, according to the school."

Calvin snorted.

"They're trying to make you guys look like a small band of kooks," Earl said.

Calvin didn't respond.

"They said the school is in touch with you guys. Who exactly are they talking to?"

Again, no response from Calvin.

"Is it you?"

"Don't ask so many questions."

"Oh, excuse me. I've only been cooped up in this office without food or water. I'm starting to feel like a hostage."

Calvin breathed heavily through his nose. He sat up. "I'm sorry," he said. "I'm sorry you had to get trapped in this. I know it's not something you care about."

"Why do you say that?"

Calvin downed half his beer in one fell swig.

"Tell me, Calvin."

"Because I know you're only out for yourself. You're out for your A, your scholarship, your ticket to Europe." He dug a cigarette from his shirt pocket and lit it with the last remaining match in a book. "Or you're only out to get into my pants," he went on. "Not because of me or anything, but just because you like big black dick. Everything you do is all about you."

"Like you're so different?" Earl said. "Like I was ever anything more to you than a hole?"

Calvin balked. "As if you didn't love it."

"As if you didn't."

Earl turned away. Getting dressed down by Rasmussen was bad enough, now Calvin was in on the act. He had hardly suspected he was so transparent. And yet, as painfully exact as their assessments of him seemed, Earl knew they were not seeing him with total clarity.

Greatness was often misunderstood to be selfishness, so Ralph Waldo Emerson thought. Earl was sure that neither Calvin nor Rasmussen had ever encountered greatness before. Therefore, they did not recognize it when they saw it.

He was so caught up in these thoughts that it took him a moment to notice what he was staring at on the TV screen—a familiar grainy image, Althus, that tape of Henry Althus making that stupid speech upstate somewhere, the tape that had been played over and over and which everyone had come to know, where he wears a multicolored kufi cap and his right arm keeps stabbing at the podium and the spittle shoots from his mouth as his rhetoric crescendos. In covering the takeover, the TV station couldn't resist digging that up. The picture changed to a young black woman who tilted her head as she talked. Behind her a police cruiser moved carefully through the crowd, which looked massive. She was identified as a student. Earl leaned forward and turned up the volume.

...sometimes you have to take action. Sometimes action is the only thing people understand. The protesters are heroes. Every single one of us is indebted to them..."

Calvin said, "The students are with us."

Earl nodded. He said, "It's the police you have to worry about."

"We're not scared of the police."

"This thing would be over in a second if they decided to move in."

"Yeah, well, if they do then we'll fight them. We'll chain ourselves to the doors."

"The point is they've decided not to move in. They're holding back."

Calvin went silent.

"The mayor doesn't want anything to do with this. He's afraid of it turning into another Althus, with the lawsuits and all the bad press. This is an election year, you know."

Calvin squinted at him but Earl never took his eyes from the TV. "How do you know all this?" Calvin said.

"I've done nothing but monitor the TV and radio since you left."

"And the mayor actually came out and said that?"

"Of course not! You have to read between the lines, Calvin. You have to listen to what's not being said."

"And how did you learn to do that?"

"By paying attention. Plus, I am a politics major."

"You have a pretty cunning mind," Calvin said, a smile cracking his tired face.

"It's not cunning, Calvin. It's critical thinking. And it seems to me you've got to be pretty sneaky to do what you guys are pulling off," said Earl, although he wasn't at all sure how much Calvin had to do with the actual planning of the takeover.

Calvin went through several more beers as he listened to everything Earl had heard—and not heard—from the media. He then abruptly yawned and laid back into the sleeping bag. Earl climbed in behind him and for the first time they had sex in a horizontal position. Calvin seemed to take pains not to aggravate Earl's hurt knee. Earl thought he was almost sensual—the way he caressed with his rough fingertips, the way he spoke to him in warm wet whispers. It was hard to make out everything he said, but Earl felt sure he heard the phrase "I love you" and that seemed to have a transcendent effect on him.

Later Earl was content to be enveloped by the feel and sweet smell of him and Calvin together. He was surprised to find how that made everything going on around him matter a great deal less than it had. Not just the takeover, but also his aspirations. There was a great relief in that The Great Plan and everything else had been put on indefinite hold.

Eventually they were startled awake by an outburst from Calvin's walkie-talkie. Again, Earl could not make it out while Calvin seemed to understand it perfectly. "I have to go," he said, jumping up.

"What? Where?" Earl was trying to wake up as quickly as he could. "What's wrong?"

"I'm needed."

"How can you understand that walkie-talkie?"

"I have to take it up to the roof. It only really works up there. Then I have other things I have to do."

"When will you come back?"

"I don't know."

"But you will come back, right? You're not going to forget about me again?"

He tucked his shirttails into his pants, leaned over and quickly kissed Earl on the lips. "I didn't forget about you before." Then he left.

Alone again, Earl hopped over to Calvin's chair and sat back. His knee was feeling a bit better. Calvin had left a half-smoked pack of cigarettes on the desk. Earl shook one out and lit it with a lighter he found in the top drawer of the desk. He utilized a bottle cap as an ashtray. He heard Muni mentioned on the radio, which he had turned up, and he leaned in to hear:

...some are saying there are not just students inside the buildings, but employees of Muni as well, although who they might be and in what capacity they might be employed is something that is not known at this time...

Sonia Rasmussen had done nothing but cry since the start of the takeover. She sat slumped on a sleeping bag that had been rolled out for her on the cafeteria floor, scarcely conscious of the activity around her as the sobs racked her body. There were brief lulls when she calmly considered that this was what it was like to have your life fall apart, and then the next convulsion would mercilessly take hold and twisted her insides like a wet dishrag.

The several other people in the cafeteria ignored her at first. They had a lot to do. They were making peanut butter sandwiches for delivery throughout the building. Ostensibly in charge was a muscular black man in army fatigues and a muscle shirt. People called him Anthony. He may have been more in charge in his head than actually. He was not always there, but when he was he strode around observing. The others were either silent or openly joked with him about his militaristic mien. He seemed to take the jokes in stride before disappearing again.

Eventually, Sonia was approached by Isabel. She had long dark hair pulled back into a ponytail except for a few strands hanging over each temple. She put a sandwich and a warm coke in front of Sonia.

"Thank you," Sonia said in a scratched-up voice. "But I'm not hungry."

"Doesn't matter," Isabel said. "You have to eat anyway. Either that or die."

Sonia looked at the meal. The sandwich was

loosely covered in see-through wrap, brown peanut butter and white marshmallow spread squishing from spots between the mushy slices of bread. She wouldn't have minded the coke, her throat was so sore, but she was not sure she had the strength to crack it open.

Isabel said, "I hope you don't mind my asking, but what's the matter with you?"

"Nothing," Sonia said absurdly.

"Then why are you crying? I mean, if you aren't here to help, then why are you here?" A pertinent question, if a painful one. She could have said, "Well, I really had nothing to lose." But instead she only muttered, "Calvin…"

"Calvin?"

"He asked me to help…"

It certainly wasn't the first time she'd allowed herself to be swayed by Calvin Reynolds.

He had shown up wanting to register late for a class of hers her first year at Muni. The class was already too big and she didn't want to make it bigger, but she relented. Why, she wasn't sure. There was something in his easygoing demeanor, his earnestness. He had that blend of dignity and flirtatiousness that was often called charm. Not to mention that he was easy on the eyes. And he turned out to be a thoughtful addition to the classroom conversation.

But that was only when he was actually there. She was dismayed to find he had a penchant for being absent. Toward the end of the semester, he started showing up in class again, clearly with no idea what had transpired in the course. But she ended up explaining to him about the required paper and when it was due. He managed to hand it in—it wasn't bad for a rush job—and though she never saw him again that semester, she passed him with an extremely generous and wholly unearned B.

All of that came back to her when he came knocking on her office door—how many hours or days ago, she didn't know—to ask her about helping with the takeover.

She had clashed with Earl not long before, and she had already pretty much put it out of her mind.

She nursed a clear plastic cup of an inexpensive champagne bought in the sincere belief—revealed now as a pathetic delusion—that everything would work out the way she wanted and she would get her tenure. In her other hand was a brown prescription bottle with fifteen, maybe twenty little white tranquilizers. It would serve them right, she thought, for them to find her lifeless body slumped at the desk.

When she didn't answer his knocks, Calvin opened the door just enough to poke his head in. "Sonia? Hi, it's me—Calvin Reynolds? I saw the light under your door. I hope you don't mind."

She slipped the pills into her pocketbook under the desk. She told him to come in, making no effort to hide the booze.

She had seen Calvin here and there in the years since he was her student. He was always nice to her.

He eyed the gold bucket on the floor next to her desk. The ice was melting into a cloudy pool around the bottom of the bottle.

"How are you doing?" Calvin said.

"Great," said Sonia.

"I heard about the committee's decision."

"Word travels."

"They should have given you tenure. They screwed you over big-time."

"Calvin, please…"

"You're a great teacher."

"No, I'm not."

"Yes, you are. You help the students. You go out of your way to help them. You helped me."

She leaned forward and started to cry, something she'd never done in front of a student before. Calvin bent down and put his arm across her back. "Hey," he said. "It's alright. Let it out." When it appeared her sobbing would not stop, he said, "Sonia. Listen to me. There's a way. There's a way you might be able to do something." She looked up at him without leaning back into her chair. The hollows under her eyes were filled with thick, slimy tears. "You have to promise me though," Calvin went on, "that you won't tell a soul what I'm about to tell you, no matter what."

She was almost on her knees in front of him. "I promise," she said.

He was selective about what he revealed of the takeover plan, but it was enough to draw Sonia temporarily out of herself. She was practically gaping by the time he said, "That's why you should join us."

She sat back in her chair. "You're…taking over the school?"

"Yes. And you have no idea how valuable you would be. A professor. On our side."

"But Calvin, they're firing me!"

"Well, maybe, if we're successful, the tenure committee might change their mind."

"Why would they do that?"

"Because you'd be some kind of folk hero around here. Like Henry Althus, in a way. There'd be no way they could let you go. It would look like you're being fired for being involved in the takeover."

Perhaps that was far-fetched. Perhaps that was a handsome young man spinning fantasies before her slightly inebriated eyes. Perhaps there was also nothing for her in the outside world but an empty apartment in Yonkers with bars on the windows and cheap floor tiles that would not stay adhered to the floor.

So she agreed to go along with what Calvin proposed.

But things had not gone smoothly. Neither she nor Calvin had bargained on her utter uselessness. He dropped her off in the cafeteria ostensibly to help with the sandwiches, saying it would be good for her to focus on something small at first. Even that proved too much for her.

Isabel rolled her eyes and turned to go as Sonia started crying again.

"Wait…" Sonia fought for some composure. "Has Calvin been around?"

"I haven't seen him since he dropped you off here."

"He said he would come back."

"Are you and him, like…together?"

"What? Why would you say that?"

"Because it seems like you are. I hear you crying and sometimes it sounds like, I don't know, the kind of crying a person does when they get their heart broken."

"I'm a teacher and he's a student," Sonia said.

"I know."

Before she left, Isabel added, "You should stay away from Calvin Reynolds. He's a total player. Everybody knows that."

Whether Isabel's was the voice of experience or not, there was something that sounded definitive in her declaration.

Sonia's appetite had returned a little. She picked up the sandwich Isabel left and noticed the plastic wrap nibbled through and a portion of one corner eaten. At first she was repulsed. Then she just tore off the part touched by the mouse's snout and ate the rest.

Daniel Scott

PART II

April 29, 1988

Daniel Scott

8

In Calvin's windowless office, day and night had ceased to exist.

Earl's every moment was spent now in a sort of reverie that perpetuated itself with no conscious effort on his part.

He kept meticulous track of who was saying what in the media, typing it all up on Calvin's electric typewriter. As usual, he found that writing it all down helped him make sense of it.

He sipped beer sparingly and ate junk food. Occasionally Calvin brought him a peanut butter sandwich. Out of sheer boredom he smoked cigarettes. He found they made him less overtly sick the more he used them. Now and again one would turn his stomach sour or make his head pound and he would stop for a while. But Calvin's stash of them in the bottom drawer of the file cabinet meant there was an endless supply.

They were sufficing with minimal washings at the basin in the hallway, but still the room was redolent with their sweat, their semen, their very breath. When they laid down in the sleeping bag, their clammy skins seemed to meld wherever they touched, and they took in one another's hot, smoky, beery vitality.

Calvin was gone sometimes for very long stretches. But he always returned to Earl, to get the latest news and to bed down with him.

Earl loved the way Calvin smiled now when he came into the office. And Earl loved the way Calvin trusted him now, how he listened with such attention to the things Earl had to say, how he laughed when he cracked a joke.

Earl's knee was back to normal, but any thought of him leaving had fallen by the wayside.

It was easy to believe this could go on forever.

He did from time to time flash on the quixotic recklessness of what he was doing after four years of virtually no missteps. He realized The Great Plan was in jeopardy before this takeover business ever started, thanks to Rasmussen. Whenever he dwelled on it too deeply, it began to pain him.

But now he could focus on what Calvin insisted on all along: that winning was possible for the protesters. Earl did not yet have a clear picture of the path to victory, but he had an overwhelming sense that it was within reach if they wanted it badly enough and worked for it hard enough.

By now Earl had been able to figure out that Calvin was not one of the leaders of the takeover, but more a second-tier lieutenant. Whoever the real leaders were, they appeared to be in one of the other seized buildings, not Fripp.

He knew that the observations he was making to Calvin regarding the takeover were being repeated by Calvin to these people. He liked to think he was helping Calvin's status among the organizers, especially since the big coup Calvin thought he had engineered—bringing Professor Sonia Rasmussen into the fold—had been such a disaster.

That night, as Calvin settled into the sleeping bag, he cut an overripe apple in two with a pocketknife and shared it with Earl. He wanted to know what was being said now on the TV.

Earl consulted his notes.

"It's what they're not saying that worries me," he said. "It's been eight days since the takeover started and it's becoming old news. Today there was nothing more than a mention. Tomorrow, at this rate, there'll be nothing at all. It worries me."

"Why?"

"Because attention is what we're going for, Calvin. This whole takeover is one big attention-getting stunt, right? The attention is what's going to force the school to do what we want."

And there was more. One of the few comments he had heard while trolling up and down the radio dial was on a local talk show. A caller who claimed to have inside knowledge of the situation said the police and the school were planning to "move in now and take drastic measures." The guy was a loudmouth who thought all the protesters should be both expelled and arrested, but Earl couldn't help wonder what "drastic measures" might mean. It was that threat that helped to push along an idea he had germinating.

"Rasmussen," he said.

Calvin stopped in mid-chew, resuming slowly. "What about her?" he said.

"It's like you told everyone at the beginning: as a faculty member, she could be very useful."

Calvin finished off a beer, then wiped his beard with his hand. It had grown out in the passing days, making his face appear softer and fuller, and showing a few traces of gray on his chin. "That's what I said," he said, "but that's not the way it's worked out."

"What's she been doing all this time?"

"Not much. Except crying. From what I hear."

"You have to talk to her, Calvin. You have to tell her to pull herself together."

"What do you think she's going to do for us anyway, Earl?"

Earl pulled a folded sheet of paper out of his shirt pocket and handed it to Calvin.

"What's this?"

"It's a speech I typed up. I want you to take this to your higher-ups, whoever they are, and tell them that we need Rasmussen to read it. Just tell them you wrote it. We need her to go on the roof with a bullhorn and read it. I saw an old bullhorn in the maintenance room. It'll be on every front page and on every news show."

Calvin read it, then folded the paper into

fourths and pocketed it.

"This is nice but I don't think I can get Sonia to read it."

"Make her do it."

"And how am I supposed to do that?"

"I don't care. Flatter her. Cajole her. Intimidate her. Threaten her." They both started to laugh. Of course Earl was only half-kidding. "Seriously, Calvin. She has to do it."

"I'll talk to her."

They were bold enough to look into one another's eyes and not flinch.

"I was wrong about you, you know," said Calvin. "You do care." He kissed Earl and they held each other tightly, almost as if they were trying to enter into one another's bodies. In the rush Earl forgot for the moment about everything else—the takeover, The Great Plan, Bertram, the omnipresent fear of getting AIDS. They made love with more tenderness than ever. In the heat of it, Earl drew himself up to Calvin's ear and said, "I'm in love with you, Calvin Reynolds."

Calvin murmured something back.

"What?" Earl said.

"I love you too," he said.

When it was over, Calvin fell asleep quickly. Earl lay there, enveloped. He realized that he had never been this happy before drifting off himself.

In the cafeteria, when daylight broke, the brown paper that covered the massive windows filtered a dirty light that Sonia thought made everyone appear bloodless and faded. She had to squint to see the person approaching her.

"Sleep well?" Isabel said.

"I guess I did." Exhaustion had finally gotten the best of her.

"It certainly sounded like you did."

"Oh." She remembered the many times her ex-husband complained about her snoring. "Sorry."

"It's okay. Look, do you think maybe you could pitch in around here a little?" Isabel said.

"Sure." Sonia was still prone to tears but grateful for the distraction.

They sat together in one of the alcoves. Sonia spread peanut butter onto bread with a plastic knife that was not really up to the job. She kept getting it on her fingers and licking it off. She folded the slices in half, wrapping them in swatches of already used plastic wrap, and tucked them neatly into a small basket that Isabel said she'd brought from home.

Sonia looked around. It seemed they were the only ones in the cafeteria for the time being.

"Where are the others?" she said.

"Some people had to get reassigned."

"Why?"

"Because some people left."

"Left?" She'd been thinking of herself as barricaded inside an impenetrable fortress.

"They smashed a window back in the kitchen and climbed through it. Didn't you hear all the commotion?"

"No."

"You must have been really tired."

"Why would people leave?" Sonia said.

"Well, you know, it's a lot of fun at first. After a while, it gets hard. Some people aren't so enthusiastic when things get hard."

They worked in silence awhile. Then Isabel said, "You know, when I first heard one of the professors was joining us, I thought, like, wow."

Sonia didn't respond.

"Then I thought, why would she do that? I mean, isn't she probably gonna get fired for this?"

Again Sonia was quiet.

"But I understand it now. You're doing it out of love."

Sonia looked and saw Isabel smiling.

"There's nothing going on between Calvin and me, Isabel," she said.

"I'm not knocking you for it," Isabel said. "I think it's kind of romantic. I just wish, for your sake, it wasn't Calvin. I can't tell you how many women I've seen him go through."

"Isabel," Sonia said, "please believe me when I say there's nothing going on between him and me."

"Oh. Okay." Isabel's eyes fluttered downward.

Sonia had seen that look before, the look of being unable to look in someone's eyes because you believed they were lying.

Gretchen Stephensen, the Dean at Mount Holyoke College, had looked at her exactly the same way when she called her in during her last year of graduate work to ask if there was "anything inappropriate" going on between her and Peter Vell, her dissertation advisor.

"Certainly not!" she had said, wondering if she sounded shocked enough.

Vell was less than twenty years her senior. She

believed that if they were dating in non-academic life, no one would have thought twice about it.

He was considered to be charismatic and adored by his students, as well as unapologetically ambitious. He was writing his first book, a lengthier version of his own dissertation on the minutiae of everyday life in the Thirteen Colonies. He had come across documents that repeatedly referenced some rather bizarre sexual shenanigans, some involving prominent members of the community, even a certain colonial governor. He believed it blockbuster material, and he already had a literary agent, a friend from his days as a Yale undergraduate. He was angling for this book to launch him into the big time. And to make him rich.

Sonia was intoxicated by his ambition and his graying temples. She was inflamed and alarmed by how much he desired her, even though she was striking in her younger days and used to the attentions of men. She recalled their first years together as if she had only been intermittently conscious during them.

Dean Stephensen went on: "Well, I hope there is nothing going on between you two. That would be a major conflict of interest on the part of Professor Vell. Not to mention an egregious violation of school statutes." Sonia watched as her mouth twitched after each sentence. Peter had told her that the Dean was out to get him ever since he was hired over a woman candidate who was a friend from her Dartmouth days.

On campus, they had been careful never to let on that they were a couple, but someone spotted them holding hands at a weekend fair in the Berkshires, where they had gone expressly to avoid being seen. Now, on the radar of the Dean, they resolved not to be seen together in public at all until the school year was over, which wasn't easy considering that they were practically living together. In addition to her own dissertation, she had been working on his book as his research assistant. They spent fevered weekends holed up in Peter's apartment, ordering in their food, writing and rewriting, and breaking now and then to eat and have sex.

Sonia believed now that those times were the high point of their relationship. She had not felt so giddily unrestrained since she was a ten-year-old barreling down a snowy Connecticut hillside barely clutching her sled and laughing crazily as she barely missed tree after tree. Just before the bottom of the hill, she hit a hidden rock and she and the sled flew off in different directions. She was laughing as she tumbled through the air, landing directly in a six-foot snowdrift. It was only afterward—when the people rushed toward her, when the terrified look on her mother's face silenced her laughter, when she looked up the hillside and saw all those trees—that she realized how close she had come to death. After that first taste of her own mortality, she never laughed that hard or that freely again.

A few months later, Sonia successfully defended her dissertation, though it was not a pretty sight. She and Peter had spent most of their time on his project. He had done very little "advising" on hers, and it suffered as a result. She stumbled over every answer, nearly coming to tears. In the end, it was Peter who just barely pulled her through. Afterward, Sonia often thought that he never regarded her quite the same way again.

Their later years were markedly different. Peter's book came out. It was well-received and drew the attention he desired. He was interviewed by *The New York Times* and *The Today Show*. He snared a National Book Award nomination, having graduated from Yale with one of the judges. PBS expressed interest in a miniseries. He parlayed the book's success into a tenure-track position at Princeton, where he only had to teach half as much as he had at Mount Holyoke. Peter used his pull to get Sonia an adjunct class or two to teach per semester. She was not at all comfortable teaching, but she did not feel she could turn the offer down. She stumbled and forgot facts, or else ended up reading to the class for forty-five minutes. She received tepid evaluations from her fellow teachers and the students. She fought terror and inertia every time she had to step into a classroom. She found herself starting to daydream a different life for herself.

She and Peter had talked a little about having children, but the conversation always ended with a decision that that "was for later." Then the matter would be abruptly dropped. But one morning, as Sonia sat at the kitchen table trying to read through a stack of essay exams, she decided that she wanted to be pregnant and would not tell Peter that she was trying. "The pill is not 100% effective," she could say.

She began to dream of the day when she could tell him she was having his baby. She dreamed of a son in whom she could instill great pride and respect for his father. She'd teach him how special it was too be the son of the great scholar Peter Vell. She dreamed, too, that the son was just as brilliant and destined for greatness as the father, and of the pride she'd take in having been the one to bring him into the world.

But, despite stopping her use of birth control pills, she never got pregnant. As time wore on, she became more alarmed about this. She saw a doctor, also without mentioning it to Peter. The news was not good and she was devastated. She was told she showed signs of once having an infection that caused irreversible damage to her ovaries. The doctor said she likely got the infection from a bout with a sexually transmitted disease. She still kept it to herself, but she was angry at Peter for not noticing her pain.

Eventually she decided it didn't matter, and that she was lucky to have him.

One afternoon she said, "Do you remember my friend Lisa from Mount Holyoke?"

He looked up from his *New York Times* and said "You mean the spinster?" He called her that because, even as a college student, that's what she looked like.

"She called a couple of weeks ago and asked me to come for a visit," Sonia said. "I think I'm going to go see her this weekend."

"Okay. If that's what you want to do."

"She's still living in western Massachusetts. I think it would be a nice drive."

"Okay, Sonia."

She drove up from Princeton. During the trip, she said things to herself, imagining she was saying them to Lisa. She imagined it would be good to talk to someone about what's been happening to her. She had confided in Lisa before (she was the only person she dared tell about her relationship with Peter while in college) and Lisa had confided in her (she was a lesbian). Lisa was not as bookish-looking as in their college days. She had lightened her hair, and let it grow out some. Around her hung an air of hostility that was not there before.

She was living in a spacious one-bedroom apartment. She made no reference to how she was making a living, but Sonia knew her family had money.

"I've given up on love," she said, like some might announce that they've changed jobs or decided to move.

"Oh," Sonia said. "Why is that?"

"Because every time I've fallen in love in my life it's been a disaster." She detailed a couple of affairs she'd had the last few years.

"That doesn't mean there's not someone out there for you."

"I don't care if there is or there isn't. The fact is, I don't think anyone is in love. I think there's a lot of self-delusion going around."

Sonia was saddened to find this new sourness in Lisa. It made things to talk about hard to come up with. And Sonia ended up not saying anything about what she had come to talk about. She was supposed to stay for three days but decided to go home in the middle of the second day. She felt more relieved than anything as she hugged Lisa and then drove off. She realized she didn't feel as bad as before, because she knew she had Peter waiting for her.

On the way back to Princeton, she decided to stop in Manhattan and do a little shopping. She bought new clothes for herself only once in a great while, but Peter always complemented her when she did. But while in the women's department at Macy's looking through the blouses, her eyes were suddenly drawn up. Why she wasn't sure, but there was something extremely familiar in her midst, a way of walking perhaps, maybe a way of pushing his hair up from his eyes.

Peter walked directly past her. Holding his hand was a young woman, attractive, fuller in the hips than the breasts, just like Sonia. She was carrying in her other hand a purchase in a small Macy's bag.

Sonia and Peter's marriage did not last much longer. Toward the end, Sonia applied for an Assistant Professorship at The Municipal University, attracted by the tenure. She did not have much experience, but she did have the last name of Vell.

She was initially well-liked by the others on the faculty, mostly because of her husband. She perhaps came off as a bit imperious, like she thought she was too good for Muni. She sometimes let on that she was a little appalled by the lacks of the place.

Relationships deteriorated quickly.

The course catalogue had listed her name as simply "Rasmussen." She went to the chair and asked it to be changed to "Rasmussen-Vell." The chair said next semester she would be sure the "Vell" was put in. What about this semester, Sonia wanted to know. The chair looked at her. There was nothing she could do, she said, since the catalogues were already printed up.

That was her first mistake at Muni, but it was by no means her worst.

She and Isabel finished making the peanut butter sandwiches. Sonia wished there were more to make. She asked Isabel if she could deliver them with her. Isabel refused, saying, "I think you'll probably want to stay here."

"Why?"

Isabel nodded her head in the direction of the doorway, where Calvin was standing.

9

For days now Bertram had kept vigil in the apartment. His soundtrack all along had been the same as Earl's—the nonstop chatter of the TV or radio, sometimes both at the same time.

During what was his day's sole excursion from the apartment, he bought *The Times, The Post* and *The News* and the city edition of *Newsday*. When they were available he grabbed *The Observer* and *The Voice* and even *The Jewish Daily Forward*. He hurried home, thinking Earl could be trying to reach him at that very moment, but the red light on the answering machine that sat near the phone was never blinking when he got back. Habitually he checked the phone to make sure there was a dial tone.

He scoured the papers for any information on

the takeover. He felt a relief when he finished an article that it had not mentioned the name of Earl Castle.

He noticed there was less to read about every day, and this morning the least of all. He gathered the papers into a neat stack that he left by the door.

He was tired. His skin was sallow. The white hair that ringed his skull was sticking out in all sorts of directions. He had developed a rather sour odor. He had not taken a shower, not because he was afraid to miss any call that might be from Earl, but because it was only him alone in the apartment. What did it matter? The last time he forsook personal hygiene was after Jo died. After several weeks of that, he began to fear for himself and started cleaning up. But he—and the apartment—never really got back to a state of normalcy until Earl had moved in.

Every call that came in he answered on the first ring. When the caller wasn't Earl, he hurried them off the line. The only exceptions were when Walt called and one call that came in that morning.

The woman's voice—"Earl, please," was all it said—was not familiar to him at first.

"Who's this?" Bertram said.

"This is his mother."

"Oh. Colleen…"

Colleen had called the apartment maybe twice in the four years Earl had been living there. Bertram was not sure how much contact they had with each other beyond that. The distance between Colleen and Earl was unlike anything Bertram had ever witnessed between a mother and her child. It made Colleen and Jo's relationship look positively warm. On Christmases and birthdays a card would show up in the mail, a check for fifty or a hundred dollars inside. Earl would fold the check and stick it in his wallet and drop the card into the trash. On Colleen's first birthday after Earl moved in, Bertram encouraged him to give her a call. Earl resisted at first, saying he did not want to talk to her.

"Earl," Bertram said reproachfully, "whatever else may be the case, she's still your mother."

"I don't need you to remind me of that," Earl had said. It recalled for Bertram how such calls left Jo in a similarly bad way, and he didn't bring it up again.

Bertram did wonder, however, about the effect

of such a mother on a child. Earl was pretty clear-eyed about Colleen, but he never let on about how much like her he was in some ways.

"Are you screening his calls for him now?" Colleen said.

"Of course not. But Earl's not here at the moment, Colleen."

"Where is he?" she said. Apparently she knew nothing of the takeover. Earl always said Colleen did not put much stock in things that had no direct bearing on her and so she was not a person who paid attention to the news. Jo had told him that Colleen's world consisted mostly of waiting around for things like funerals and weddings to happen.

"I'm not exactly sure where he is."

"When will he be back?"

"I really couldn't say."

"Well you're just a wealth of information."

"I wish I could be more helpful, Colleen." He could hear her drawing air through her nostrils in the way that Jo always hated.

An ache was starting just behind his eyes. "Maybe you want to leave a message?" he said.

"It's really a family matter."

Bertram felt stung.

"But you can tell him that his Uncle Vaughn died."

"Oh, no."

"The funeral is Saturday. I still have his black suit here."

"I'm sorry," he said. "I'm so sorry." Even his memory of what a funeral was like in that family did not dampen how sorry he felt to hear this news. "I'll tell him," he said, "if I see him."

"If you see him?" she said.

"Well, he hasn't been around a lot lately." Immediately he knew he said too much.

"Oh really?" Colleen said. "And just where has he been?"

"All I mean is, he usually spends most of his time at school at the end of the semester."

"Please leave a message for him to call me," she said.

"I will," Bertram said. And before Colleen could hang up, he said, "Was this someone Earl was very close to?"

"Excuse me?"

"I'm just wondering—since I have to tell him about it—how close they were."

"He's Earl's uncle," she said.

"I know, but...did they know each other very well?"

"What difference does that make?"

"Maybe none. I don't know." He was getting dizzy.

"Do I have to assume that you're planning not to tell Earl about his uncle's passing?"

"No. I'll tell him. If I see him."

"Which means you may not get around to it?"

That was not what Bertram meant.

"I knew it was a mistake, him moving in with you," she said.

"Now, Colleen..."

"I knew you'd do nothing but fill his head with lies about me. I knew you'd try to turn him against me."

"I didn't do that, Colleen. You did it all by yourself."

"First you steal my mother from me and then my son! Well, let me tell you something: no matter how much you try to do for him, no matter what happens, Earl will never be your son!"

Bertram had done a good job up until then of keeping his anger in check. But now she had gone too far. Bertram did not think of Earl as his son. Bertram had a son, once. He knew what it was like. He did not have to imagine it through Earl.

"Well, let me tell you something, Colleen. If Earl was my son, I sure as hell wouldn't treat him like some piece of dog shit that got stuck to my shoe. I wouldn't be so wrapped up in myself that I couldn't see how gifted he was—and how that gift deserves to be respected and nurtured!"

There was a spluttering at the other end of the line. No one had talked to Colleen that way for a very long time.

"You! You don't know what you're talking about!"

"Unfortunately for you, I do!"

"You, you're an old Jew!"

"Here it comes! Earl told me you hated me because of that!"

"I don't hate you because of that. I just hate you!"

"Goodbye, Colleen."

"Don't think for one minute that this is the end of this."

"Goodbye, Colleen." He hung up. He took a deep breath. He held his head in his hands, trying to keep the room from moving.

He chastised himself. It was Walt who told him once that arguing with an idiot made you the bigger idiot.

Sometime later, it was with alarm that Bertram awoke to find himself sleeping on the living room recliner. The last thing he remembered was feeling dizzy immediately following the phone argument with Colleen.

Insistent knocks at the door were what had woken him up.

He got up with some difficulty. A peep through the glass hole in the door told him it was Jesse, the super. Standing next to him was a bald man in a rumpled coat with wide lapels. He unlocked and opened the door. Jesse smiled in his sheepish way. The bald man asked if he was Bertram Berg. He produced a leather wallet out of which he flipped a police badge and a picture I.D. All Bertram could make out was that his name Hodges and at one time he had more hair and a dark moustache.

"Is Earl Castle here?" he said.

Bertram looked at Jesse, who was making signals that he needed to get back to work.

Hodges, meanwhile, slipped into the apartment

without being invited. His eyes were drawn to the rooms he could not see into.

Bertram believed you should always make nice with police officers. They didn't make much money, and they were all a little crazy to begin with. Even the ones in suits. "Maybe I can help?"

"I'd like to ask Mr. Castle a few questions about the Municipal University takeover."

"Earl wouldn't know anything about that."

"Where is he right now?"

"I'm not really sure."

"We traced a call that came from inside the school to here on the first morning of the takeover," the detective said.

Bertram sank silently into a chair at the table.

"I thought the police weren't getting involved. I mean, that's what I heard on TV."

"We're only involved in an off-the-record kind of way, for now. It was Earl who called you from the college. Isn't that right, Mr. Berg?"

"I don't recall. I mean, I don't remember getting a call from any college."

"Mr. Berg, we know the call came in. It lasted almost four minutes."

"Is a crime being investigated?"

"That's still to be determined. I'm just trying to find out some information."

"Do you think any of those kids will be arrested?"

"Like I said, that's still to be determined."

"They're not criminals."

"Maybe not. Who does Earl hang out with? Who are his friends?"

"I don't know."

"Mr. Berg…"

"I'm telling you I don't know. As far I as know, Earl doesn't have any friends."

"I find that a little hard to believe."

"That's because you don't know Earl," Bertram said, and indeed, since this whole takeover business started some part of him had been trying to reconcile the Earl he knew with the person presently holed up in Muni. But his first instinct was to protect Earl. He did not want to see any harm come to the boy. More than that, he wanted him to succeed and fulfill his potential.

"What did Earl say when he called you?" Hodges said.

"I don't know what you're talking about. No one ever called me."

"You're lying, Mr. Berg."

"No, I'm not."

"We have the phone record."

"It must have been a wrong number."

"Four minutes is awfully long for a wrong number, Berg."

"Oh so it's 'Berg' now? So now you're dispensing with the niceties? Well, what are you going to do, Detective? Are you going to rough up a 68-year-old man? Is that what will make you look good to the people who sent you?"

"Nobody's going to rough up anybody. But you will make it harder on yourself if you don't cooperate. You can send me away if you want to. But I can't guarantee that the next person who shows up here is going to be as reasonable with you as I'm being. You could save yourself a lot of aggravation if you simply tell me who called you from the school and what they said."

It seemed inevitable that the detective would find out what he wanted to know. But he was not going to hear it from Bertram Berg.

Once that became clear, Hodges said, "Have it your way." He flicked a business card at Bertram and said, "In case your memory improves."

Bertram locked both locks after he left.

For a moment he stood with his back to the door. It was almost unfathomable to him how spectacularly Earl's dreams were crashing down all around him.

In the frosted vessel next to the door, he spied the envelope addressed to Earl. He picked it up and sat at the table. He had torn it open already, and looked at what it said. The valedictorian committee had been deeply impressed with him at the initial interview—until he read the letter, Bertram had known nothing about any interview —and they would like him to come in for a second interview. With Muni closed down, the date had already come and gone.

Later, when Walt called after the evening news like he always did, Bertram told him about Hodges, and how the police and no doubt the school were on to Earl. "The jig is up," he said. "The cat's out of the bag."

"We don't know that yet," Walt said. "Your voice sounds weak, Bert. You're exhausting yourself over this."

"No, I'm not."

"Are you eating, Bert?"

"Yes."

"But not very much."

"Not very much."

So Walt invited himself over, saying he'd bring Chinese takeout and his old cribbage board.

"Don't come," Bertram said.

"I'm coming," said Walt.

Daniel Scott

10

The waiting itself Earl didn't mind. He rather liked it. The slow passing of long minutes was restful in its way. He remembered being taken to a Yankees game when he was little, in the days before his father got sick. The rain delay was the most interesting part. The waiting for something to happen was better than the game itself.

He was also intrigued by the uninterrupted streams of thought that came—quite without his willing it—whenever he gave his ears and eyes a rest from the radio and television. His notions ranged from distant memories to very recent ones, most of which involved Calvin, to speculations about the future which also managed to be mostly about Calvin.

In any case, the worst part of waiting was that

Calvin was not there with him.

And it seemed as if Calvin's absences grew longer as his explanations grew vaguer.

His last stop to the office Calvin seemed more exhausted and irritable than he ever had. He was still up for sex, yes, but that had never been his problem. Afterward, he said he had to leave again. Earl asked when he would return and Calvin chafed at having to answer. Still, Earl pressed. Calvin finally said he'd be gone three, four hours tops.

But now more than six hours had passed, and Earl was starting to get tired of being told things he wanted to hear. He wanted some truth.

He lay back on the sleeping bag and dozed a bit.

When he opened his eyes again it was one of the most terrifying moments of his young life.

He shot up. All he could see was blackness. "I'm blind," he said. "I'm blind!" He shook his head, blinked his eyes again and again, rubbed them hard and very lightly, but there was nothing but excruciating, empty darkness.

Then he noticed something. The radio and television were no longer murmuring. And the red light that glowed on Calvin's electric typewriter was no longer there.

"They cut the power," he said to no one there.

Very carefully, like he was on a balance beam, Earl stood up. He knew he had seen a flashlight in the bottom drawer of Calvin's desk. He made his way over to it with a minimum of bumping into things, being especially careful about his nearly recovered knee. He felt around in the drawer. A stray thumbtack jabbed his finger. Finally he got his hands on the flashlight.

He turned it on. The beam of light was weak, but Earl was happy for it. He used it to search for fresh batteries. He found large ones for the television, but no small ones for radio. He loaded up the TV. He turned it on and shut the flashlight off. The radio, it turned out, had batteries in it already, though they were close to dead. He tuned it in as best he could. He leaned in to listen to any word of what was happening. Of course there was nothing. The school and the police weren't just going to announce their "drastic measures" over the air.

Where was Calvin?

He shut the radio off to conserve the battery.

He turned the volume all the way down on the television, but left the room bathed in the dancing gray light of its black-and-white picture.

He wondered, for the first time since he got there, if he should try to leave. Were the police at that very moment swarming the lower floors?

Keys jingled suddenly on the other side of the door. Earl jumped up in anticipation of Calvin, who seemed to be having difficulty opening the door. Earl pictured him hurt in some way. He hurried over and opened the door for him.

What met him were two flashlights shined in his eyes. Beyond that he could see the outlines of two people—one tall, one stockier with a bald head reflecting some small trace of light from somewhere. Earl put a hand up, shielding his eyes from the light.

"You're not Calvin," he heard a woman say. He recognized the voice from the maintenance room as Isabel's.

The muscular man called Anthony stepped up and turned the light directly on Earl's face and said, "Who the fuck are you?"

Earl tried again to shield his eyes. "I…I thought you were Calvin," he said.

The man and then the woman pushed past him into the office. "What the fuck is going on in here?" the man said, whipping the light around the office.

"You might as well turn off your flashlights," Earl said, gesturing toward the TV. "Conserve the batteries."

Isabel did just that. Anthony did not.

"I asked what was going on here," he said.

"There's nothing going on here," Earl said.

"It sure as hell doesn't look like nothing," the man said.

"Take it easy, Anthony," said Isabel. For the first time, Earl got a good look at her. She was large all around, but still young enough to be called voluptuous. Her long black hair was now piled precariously on her head. She said, "So— who are you?"

"I've been helping Calvin in here," he said.

"Where is Calvin?" said Isabel.

"I don't know. Not here."

"Of course he's not!" Anthony grabbed the walkie-talkie that was somehow secured to his belt. "Third floor is negative," he barked, "but we have an unfamiliar." There seemed to be no response.

"Talk like a normal person, Anthony," Isabel said. "They're probably not even hearing you."

"Hey, don't get mad at me just because your boyfriend skipped out on you."

"Calvin's not my boyfriend," she said. "And he didn't skip out."

"Where is he then? We looked everywhere. He's not in the building. He left with those other chicken-ass wimps. I just wish he'd left his goddam walkie-talkie and keys behind."

"I can't believe he would leave," she said.

"I can," he said. They both looked at Earl. "Just how do you and Calvin know each other?" Anthony said. "Just how have you been helping him?"

But Earl suddenly had a graver concern. He said, "Are you saying…Calvin is gone?"

"Probably home in his comfy bed by now. Either that or he's spilling his guts to the police—or the school—telling everybody everything!"

"Shut up, Anthony," Isabel said.

"Calvin was going soft. Especially in the last couple of days. Something was different about him. Like he had something to hide." He shined the light in Earl's eyes again. "You still haven't told me your name."

Earl turned his head away and said, "I can't believe Calvin would leave…"

"Neither can I," Isabel said.

"Believe it. Calvin's like that. It was the same when we were protecting Dr. Althus. Right when he was going to join us, he backed out. The man can't sustain."

"But how…?" Earl said. "How could he have gotten out?"

"Through the same rathole the others did," Anthony said.

"They smashed a window in back of the kitchen," said Isabel. "We boarded it up."

Earl went to the desk and began searching through the drawers again. He said, "How many of us are left in total?"

"It's sort of hard to tell," said Isabel.

"Give me a rough estimate. Five? Ten? A hundred?"

"A hundred?" Isabel said.

"Now wait just a minute," Anthony said. "You're not giving the orders around here."

"What are you doing?" Isabel said.

"I'm trying to find batteries for the radio. I need to know what the hell is going on. It's important that I monitor things. I have to get an idea of what they know on the outside."

"You know," Isabel said, "it would be nice if you told us who you are. I mean, neither of us has seen you before."

"I'm one of the students. I'm one of you."

"In the way Calvin was one of us?" Anthony said.

"What's your name?" Isabel said.

"I hope he's not hurt…"

Anthony stepped up and kicked shut the drawer Earl was looking into. He pulled his hand back just in time.

"The lady asked you your name?" he said. Earl looked at Isabel, who was not holding Anthony back this time.

Something inside him, some vestige of The Great Plan, was stopping him from saying his name.

"Walt," said Earl. "I'm Walt Escher."

Earl was not sure why it was Walt's name that came to him. Except to say that if he ever admired anyone in his life, if he ever met anyone that he might want to be like, Walt Escher was probably that person. He remembered the time Bertram called him to show him something he pulled from the bookcase. Earl sauntered over, trying to make out like he didn't care. "This book," Bertram said, "it's one of Walt's." Earl looked down at the book. He touched the cover. *The Most Perfect Flaw* was the title. By Walter Escher. It was a collection of essays. "You might want to read it," Bertram said. "Walt had quite an amazing career." Prior to that, all Walt had been to Earl was Bertram's weekly cribbage partner.

Anthony said to Isabel, "Don't you think it's strange that Calvin never told any of us there was someone up here with him?"

"Maybe he would have told you," Earl said, "if you didn't act like such an ass."

"Look, Walt Escher, there's about a half an inch of patience separating me from you right now."

"Alright, knock it off," Isabel said. "We've got batteries downstairs, Walt," Isabel said. "Tons of them. Any size you could want. I'll go down and get some for you."

"Thank you, Isabel," Earl said.

"Great," Anthony said. "Then Walt and me can

have ourselves a little talk."

"What's the matter with you?" Isabel said. "Can't you see that he's on our side? Don't mind Anthony, Walt. He just thinks he's in a Sylvester Stallone movie."

"Then how come no one's ever seen him before?" Anthony said.

"Like he said, he's been up here monitoring the radio!"

"And what the hell good does that do?"

"Batteries," Earl said. "I really need those batteries."

"I'll get them," said Isabel. Earl and Anthony listened to her sneakers as they squeaked down the corridor.

"You might as well sit down and relax," Earl said. "There's chips, if you want."

Anthony shook his head no.

"There's beer, if you want," said Earl.

Anthony thought on it a minute and said, "Yeah, okay."

Earl passed him one from the styrofoam cooler. Not only the ice but the water melted from the ice was long gone.

"How is she getting downstairs?" Earl said. "I

mean, aren't all the stairwells locked or blocked?"

Anthony jingled the ring of keys he had in one belt loop. "Before we were using the freight elevator to get from floor to floor, but with the power cut we had to unlock everything."

"Do you know how many people left?" Earl said.

"Not exactly."

"Or how many of us remain?"

"I really couldn't tell you."

A talking head showed up on the television screen. Underneath her were the words COMING UP AT NOON. Earl turned it up and grabbed some paper to take notes. Anthony watched him curiously. For several minutes, they listened. There was nothing about the takeover. Earl then snapped off the TV to save the batteries.

"So you're taking all kinds of notes," Anthony said. "Are you planning on writing a book, Walt?"

"No. It just helps me clarify my thoughts."

For several uncomfortable minutes they sat looking at and away from each other.

"So you and Calvin are buddies, huh?" Anthony said.

Earl ignored the remark and said, "Did you say

Calvin was involved with the Althus business?"

"Yup."

"I didn't know that."

"He probably didn't mention it because it wasn't quite his finest hour."

"Why not?"

"Because he bailed when things got a little rough. Just like now."

"What do you mean a little rough?"

"I mean when it came time to stand between the good doctor and the persons who wanted to do him harm. You see, Calvin likes the idea more than the reality. He's got a little problem on the follow-through."

Earl considered what he was just told.

"It just doesn't seem like the Calvin I know," Earl said.

"Just how do you know Calvin, Walt? You two buddies?"

"I guess. We're fighting for the same cause."

"So every night when he came up here to sleep you were here waiting for him, huh? And you two would talk about the cause together?"

"That's right."

"But then the power went out and he decided

he missed his warm, cozy bed at home. And he just left you here in the dark."

Earl sank into thought. Was that how it was? Was it really every man for himself? Had Calvin's interest in him extended only as far as the moment? He put his head down on the desk.

Earl had not given The Great Plan a great deal of thought in the past days, but now he began to turn it over in his mind again.

A knock at the door interrupted the silence they lapsed into. Earl figured it was Isabel, but then they heard, "Calvin? Are you in there?" It was a woman's voice. Earl knew instantly it was Rasmussen's. He had to fight the urge to scramble for a hiding place as Anthony got up to open the door.

Anthony let out a loud sigh when he saw who it was.

"Oh hi," Sonia said. "I heard talking. I've been looking for Calvin?"

"Join the club," Anthony said.

Rasmussen looked Earl's way. He had turned the television slightly to make his face appear darker. She showed no signs of having recognized him. He certainly, at first, labored to recognize her. She looked like a dingy, bruised, unwanted doll you might find at a landfill somewhere, only life-size.

"I've been waiting for him in my office," she said. "He left me there and told me to wait for him. I waited and waited. Then the lights went out…"

"Calvin left," said Anthony.

"What? No. You're mistaken. Calvin wouldn't leave."

Anthony rolled his eyes. "Another one," he muttered.

"But he said he would come back. He told me to wait for him. He said…"

"He lied!" Anthony said.

Sonia sort of fell back a little. Anthony looked as though he expected her to fall apart all over again, and for a moment Earl too expected to see tears. But she was managing to contain herself. She slipped a folded piece of paper from the pocket of her long skirt.

"He gave me this," she said, opening it. Earl knew it was the speech he had written for her. "He said I was supposed to read it. I'm not sure to whom."

"Well you can forget about it now," Anthony said.

"No!" Earl said, almost despite himself. He stayed seated in the half-dark. "She's right. She's supposed to read it." But what did he care? Did any of it matter now, without Calvin?

"What the hell is it?" said Anthony.

"It's a statement," she said. "Calvin wrote it. It really is wonderfully written."

Anthony took it from her and looked it over. "Calvin wrote this?"

"That's what he told me. I admit I was a little surprised to hear he wrote it. I had him once as a student and…"

Isabel arrived with the batteries. She gave them to Earl and he loaded up the radio. He said to her, "Do you know where the maintenance room on the third floor is?"

"Yes," said Isabel.

"There's an old bullhorn there. Can you get it for me?"

"Yeah, sure." She left on her task.

"Come in," he said to Rasmussen. She examined him more closely, but still did not appear to recognize him. Earl did not realize how different he looked from the last time she saw him. A beard darkened his face, his hair was tangled and in his eyes. And he was thinner, even thinner than before, and it gave his face a gaunt, hollowed-out expression. And he was in clothes given to him by Calvin that were at least three sizes too big for him.

"Hello," he ventured.

"Hi. I'm Sonia."

"I know who you are. And I know what Calvin intended you to do with that statement."

"I want to be of some help…"

"Good. I want you to go to the roof of this building and read that statement through the bullhorn," he said. "But only when you're sure the TV cameras are on you."

A look of panic came over her. "Oh, I don't think I can do that," Sonia said.

"You have to do it."

"I can't…"

"I'll do it," Anthony said.

"No!" said Earl. "It has to be her. She's the only faculty member among us."

"But I'm no good at public speaking," Sonia said.

"You said you wanted to help, right? Now's the time."

"I don't think I can memorize this."

"You don't have to memorize it. You just have to read it."

"How do you know there's going to be TV cameras there?"

"I don't know it, not for sure. But I heard on the radio there was going to be a rally at Muni today put together by a group of students who think the takeover is a bad thing." This man had had a rough, gravelly voice. He said the protesters were hurting students, not helping them. The school had been threatening to cancel the semester outright if the takeover did not end soon. The guy had been weighing on Earl ever since he heard him. He had been waiting to talk to Calvin about it.

Sonia read over the statement until Isabel returned with the bullhorn. It was in rougher shape than Earl had thought. All those times he had glanced at it while waiting for Calvin in the maintenance room, he never actually picked it up and looked at it. Anthony and Isabel fussed with it until they were finally able to secure its large battery by holding it in with masking tape.

"You'll have to be careful when you use it," Isabel said to Sonia. "Don't touch here or you could get an electric shock."

Sonia took awkward hold of the bullhorn. It was heavier than she suspected. She looked at the grimy mouthpiece that she was supposed to speak into.

"It's just about time for the noon news to start," Earl said. "If we're lucky maybe we'll get some live coverage. Now remember, you have to get the attention of the cameras before you start."

"How do I do that?" Sonia said.

"You'll think of something."

"I need someone to come with me." She looked directly at Earl, which made him fall back a bit. "I don't think I can go up there by myself."

"I can't go with you," Earl said. "I have to stay here."

"I'll go with her," Anthony piped up. Anthony's suspicion of Earl had eased somewhat, and that made everyone feel easier. Anthony grabbed his walkie-talkie. He and Sonia left for the roof.

Earl tuned in the news on the television. Isabel sat down to watch with him. She said, "Anthony isn't really as crazy as he likes to come off."

"I know."

"His heart is in the right place."

Earl nodded.

"He's just bothered by the fact he's never seen you before. And by Calvin just running out on us."

"So you think he took off, too?"

"All I know is we're here and he's not."

Earl leaned back in the chair and shut his eyes for an instant. He could still smell Calvin on him, a sweet tangy odor.

Moments later, Anthony and Sonia emerged onto the roof of the building. All around them were giant HVAC units, none of them working. Under their feet was gravel. Sonia was breathing hard from climbing the steps. Anthony, despite the great shape he was in, was a little winded, too.

They heard a deep voice talking on the wind. It wafted over their heads and wobbled, incomprehensible except for its urgency.

"Stay here," Anthony told her. He made his way to the side of the building and carefully peered down. Directly below he saw three police cars parked in a row on the red bricks. Farther out, he saw a gathered crowd, including news crews with their cameras pointed at a man with his own bullhorn. He appeared to be a student. Anthony cocked his head and caught snippets of what the guy was saying.

"...they're not helping us, they're holding us back..."

"...cancelling the semester...thousands can't graduate..."

"...just selfish...playing a game with our futures..."

Anthony pulled back and returned to Sonia.

"What's he saying?" she said.

"Some bunch of bull. But you can't start until he finishes. Like Walt said, you have to make sure the cameras are pointed at you before you start speaking."

"Is that what his name is? Walt?"

"That's what he says."

"So you don't know him," said Sonia.

"I know him about as well as I know you," Anthony said. "I think he's on the level, though. I'm a pretty good judge of people when I meet them in high-pressure situations. I was in Grenada, you know. When we invaded in '83? I was a Marine."

"Oh."

He took up his walkie-talkie and started fiddling with it. Sonia looked up at the sky, which she had not seen in a while. The breeze and the sunlight felt cleansing.

Anthony exchanged a few terse words with someone on the walkie-talkie. Then he hung it on the clip on his belt.

He said, "I think what you're doin' is aces, ya know. I think it's really brave."

"Really?"

"Yeah. It's one thing to put your ass on the line, it's another to put your job on the line."

"Oh. Well. I'm not really doing that. If anything I'm trying to save both my job and my ass."

"We all have our reasons for doing what we do."

"Do you think this is even going to work? Nobody cares who I am."

"I guess we'll find out."

They realized simultaneously that the man with the bullhorn was no longer speaking.

"It's showtime at the Apollo," said Anthony.

She followed him to the edge of the roof. She

tried not to tremble so hard.

They stood together a moment, not knowing how to make the people down there look up.

Then Anthony just started shouting. "Hey! Hey you motherfuckers! Up here! Up here! Hey stupid! Hey ugly! I'm talking to you, mister with the TV camera! HEYYYY!!!!"

The crowd and the cameras began to gather. Anthony handed Sonia the bullhorn and stepped back out of sight.

Sonia stepped up. She had never seen the campus from this perspective. It really was beautiful. She had never seen the gothic spires of the older buildings. She had never seen the Muni flag raised over Administration.

Anthony called from behind her: "Go ahead!"

She lifted the bullhorn to her mouth, but struggled to find her voice. "Excuse me," she said into the bullhorn. She pulled it away from her face, surprised at the power of it. She then tried again. "Excuse me, everybody. Can I have your attention, please? Hello?"

When it seemed as though she had everyone's attention, she looked down at the sheet of paper she had. It felt like the time she was defending her dissertation: she was nervous, weak and wondered if she could get through it without bursting into tears.

But she began.

"My name is Sonia Rasmussen-Vell and I am a professor of history here at the Municipal University of New York. I am participating in this takeover because it is the right thing to do. For too long, Muni and the other colleges in the city system have served as the sacrificial lambs whenever Albany has mismanaged itself into some or other fiscal crisis. It is time to say enough. It is time to let the governor, the mayor and the legislature know that we will no longer stand by while they shortchange the futures of our young people and our city. Every year Muni sends thousands of bright, hard-working, motivated graduates into the city's workforce. Muni has more Nobel Prize laureates than any other public institution in the nation. It takes resources to maintain excellence like that. It takes students and teachers and staff. The time has come to make a stand, and we will remain here until our demands are met."

Her voice had gained strength as she went on.

She was wielding the bullhorn with great command.

"Demand One: no increase in tuition. Don't drive out the people who need this university the most, the people who Muni's historical mission it has always been to serve.

"Demand Two: no faculty or staff layoffs. Class sizes are already too big.

"Demand Three: no budget cuts. Supplies are already stretched too thin. We've got teachers stealing each other's chalk. We've got bathrooms going without toilet paper.

"Demand Four: no cuts in financial aid.

"Those are our demands. Again, we will not come out until they are met."

She'd done it. The crowd below seemed stunned into silence. She backed from the edge of the roof and turned around. Anthony was almost beaming.

Two floors below, Earl had watched her on the one channel that carried it live. Even he had to admit it went better than he could have imagined. The talking heads were chattering away about it.

"She was great," said Isabel.

The speech was indeed listened to. It was

broadcast repeatedly on television and the radio that day. It led off the news a few hours later that a faculty member was on the inside, in on the takeover. The media focused on just who Sonia Rasmussen-Vell was. Beyond her failed marriage, there wasn't that much to find. But someone had dug up a photo of her, not a bad one, smiling, younger and blonder than she was now. It was a posed photo with another person—possibly Peter Vell—who had been cropped out. Only an arm around Sonia's shoulder showed.

The takeover was news again, just as Earl had planned.

"I have to admit I wasn't sure she had it in her," Isabel said. "I thought for sure once she found out lover boy bailed on us, she'd crack up again."

Earl looked at her questioningly.

"Oh you don't know? Her and Calvin were, like, together."

"What?" The news nearly caused him to jump from his chair. Calvin and Rasmussen? Calvin and that hideous old hag? The thought almost made him retch. His head got hot and his knee started to ache again.

"What the hell are you talking about?" he

snapped.

"Her and Calvin. There was something going on. Gross, I know."

Suddenly Earl was struggling to keep everything untangled and logical in his head as he was also trying to control the rage that was rising fast in him. "How do you know that?" he said. "Did Calvin tell you that?"

"No…"

"She told you that?"

"Not exactly. But it's obvious. I mean…"

"She's a teacher and he's a student…"

"It wouldn't be the first time, you know."

Of course that was true. Teachers and students had affairs all the time. Earl knew that. He knocked on an English professor's door once in his freshman year. He watched as the light showing under the door suddenly went off. He heard the soft talking. He walked away with an even lower opinion of the professor, whom he had written off as an idiot from the very first class.

But Calvin and that…thing?

Never had Earl felt so helpless against the scorching in his veins, a combustion of rage and pain that his intellect was useless against.

11

For a long time now, Bertram had done little but watch the news when it was on TV and listen to it when it was on the radio.

Walt had been coming over every day now, which Bertram wasn't exactly happy about. Sometimes the buzzer would go off and Bertram would have to let him in. Other times, Walt would simply show up at the door—someone on their way in or out had let him in, or Jesse the super had recognized him. Bertram only picked at the food he brought.

"Eat, Bert! What do you hope to accomplish by not eating?"

The cribbage at least engaged his mind, however undemandingly, with numbers. And Walt being there at least kept him from calling and tying up the phone line. Earl could be trying to get through any minute.

"The phone company has a thing now called call waiting," Walt informed him. "You might have heard of it? It lets you put someone on hold while you talk to someone else."

"So what am I now, the receptionist?" Bertram said.

As they played Walt would invariably get around to talking about a woman he just met, or one he was avoiding. Bertram pictured them in his mind as relatively vibrant women who were typically ten or fifteen years younger than Walt. They had medium-length hair cut in flattering fashions. They had clothes that fit well their still shapely figures. They smiled easily and cleared their throats to speak.

Bertram had to wonder where in the world Walt met all these women.

"Oh," Walt said, "they're around. They're everywhere, really."

Bertram had to go through a fairly elaborate ruse involving a fictional lost umbrella just to talk to Jo for the first time. It was not unlike the story he devised to meet his first wife, Gloria, only that time it was a wallet that was supposedly misplaced.

Some falsehood or other was inevitably involved whenever Bertram desired to speak to a woman he was attracted to, even going as far back as Lucinda Gold from his Muni days.

The first time he laid eyes on her, Lucinda was subbing at the cash register in the cafeteria while the regular lady took her lunch break. The cashier was in charge of a paper cup filled with packets of sugar. Bertram stood in line pretending to want one.

"You have to buy a coffee or tea to get one of those," Lucinda said, not hiding her smile.

"But I've got my thermos right here," Bertram had said, smiling back.

The day after the Stuckey incident, however, someone other than Lucinda was sitting in at the register, an older lady who looked a little unhuman in her hairnet.

Bertram sighed and sat at a table to wait. He had the ring on him again. He was thinking the best way to spring the question on Lucinda was casually, while they ate lunch.

Alcove number one was buzzing, but he didn't

hear Escher blasting away as usual. Instead, Marcus Rhyman was standing up and speaking, but not loud enough to hear. He looked uncomfortable up there, like he couldn't stand that people were looking at him and his teeth. He tried not to open his mouth too wide, which had a muffling effect on his words.

When he spotted Bertram nearby, he tried to engage him in the manner of Walt Escher.

"Um, excuse me," he said, "excuse me please. Sir? Hey buddy, I'm talking to you."

But Bertram didn't answer. He didn't even turn his way.

Or rather, he couldn't.

Later, when he reconstructed it in his mind, he thought that it was maybe just one of those instances when you see something really fast, just get a glimpse of it, and you think you know what you saw but you can't really be a hundred percent sure.

Directly behind the lady with the scary hairnet was a swinging door that led back to the kitchen. Someone suddenly walked through it and for an instant Bertram could see back there. And right in his line of vision was another, partly open door that looked out to the trash area behind the building. And beyond that he saw Lucinda.

With Escher.

It was only for a second and they were a good distance away, yet Bertram could see the hairs on the back of Escher's hand as it moved over Lucinda's round caboose. She had him backed against the wall. Lucinda's gold-colored hair was just starting to slip out the back of her hairnet.

Bertram stood up. He turned around and walked past the line of people holding their food trays, past the alcoves, past the folks eating at the tables. He went through the doors, through the lobby, out to the campus. He had never walked the length of the campus before, but it was very compact as campuses go and he didn't have to go all that far. He came to the stadium. There was nothing to stop him from going in. The early April air was chilly despite the shining sun. He had to shield his eyes with one hand to see the athletes on the field. Men in blue-and-white Muni shorts and shirts were throwing javelins and jumping hurdles. One was standing with a long pole in his hand. As Bertram got closer, he realized the man was watching him approach. It was Stuckey.

"Hi, buddy!" Stuckey said, his mouth turning up.

Now Bertram had never been to the stadium in all his four years at Muni. Sports were not among his interests. He'd still rather do a tax return than sit through a baseball game. He wasn't even sure how he knew where to go to find the stadium, or that the track team would be would be there that day. But there he was nodding as Stuckey talked, trying to ignore the beads of sweat that clung to the hairs on the athlete's shoulders and upper arms.

Bertram agreed to meet Stuckey later that afternoon at the corner of Convent Avenue and West 142nd Street, just a few blocks up from Muni, and only a block or so from Lucinda's normal school. Escher and his cohorts were planning some kind of event at this corner. Bertram showed up and was surprised to find Stuckey had some of his pals with them. Bertram followed them up a stairwell to the roof of an apartment building that Stuckey said was owned by his father. Being up so high—ten or eleven stories—made the neighborhood unfamiliar to Bertram. The sun was high in the sky and the air had turned steamier. The roof had a silver-white reflecting surface and Bertram began to feel like he was being baked alive.

They peeked over the side of the building to the street below. The protesters, led by Escher, had worked up a pretty good crowd below, he said. Escher was on a crate of some kind, orating while his minions went out into the crowd to distribute literature and keep things stoked. Bertram wondered what those boys thought they were going to do for a living—follow this guy around like he was Socrates? He could hear Escher running on about the ROTC on campus being akin to the German troops that had marched into Austria a month before. Bertram could see the top of Escher's head and a bit of its bald spot. Or at least he thought that was what he saw.

Bertram pulled back from the side, a little dizzied by the height. He had always been a person who had to take a good long look at something before he came to any conclusions about it. He thought about the image of Escher and Lucinda holding each other. Could he have been wrong? Could it not have been them all along? If it was them, could they have been doing something completely innocent?

But he had to admit that the most plausible conclusion was the one he had come to immediately.

Around Stuckey and his jock buddies, he pretty much felt like a pipsqueak. But somehow he believed he was necessary to help lift the bag of lime, which had stamped right on it "CALCIUM OXIDE 120 LBS." He said to himself, "So that's how big a 120-pound bag of lime is." He supposed they were going to pour it over the side and everybody would get dirty which, when he thought about it, didn't sound like much of a revenge against Escher.

But the athletes had a different idea. Stuckey motioned to Bertram to help them lift the bag of lime. He gave it his all. And he did share the elation of the others when the whole heavy bag went up in the air, basking in the hazy sunshine, seeming for an instant like it might float away. Of course it went down and over the side of the building and that was the end of any more feelings like elation. Bertram stopped breathing for long seconds, then gasped at the loud thud of the bag hitting…something.

People were screaming. People were gagging. Escher had abruptly stopped speaking.

Stuckey and his buddies all rushed to look over the side. But Bertram couldn't.

He turned and ran down the ten flights and bolted out the back door and into the alleyway. He never wanted to get away from a place so bad, but he couldn't help looking back. A thick cloud of dirty white dust floated in the air, moving in almost solid form from the street to the alley and dispersing against the red brick wall. He froze as several people stumbled from the cloud. They were coughing and they were covered in the dust. Two were men and the other was a woman— Lucinda. Her face and her fabulous hair were whited out completely but her form was unmistakable.

"Bertie?" she said, her eyes watery slits on her face.

"Are you hurt?" Bertram said.

"What are you doing here?" she said.

"What are you doing here?"

"Me and some of the girls stopped to listen to Walter Escher speak. Then all of a sudden there was an explosion, and everything turned white."

"You didn't see the bag drop?"

"The what?"

"What happened to your girlfriends?"

"I don't know."

"I better get you home."

Lucinda lived in one of the normal school's dormitories. Bertram had to stop with her at the lobby since men were only allowed that far, and then only from 9:30 a.m. to 3:45 p.m.

"You're sure you're not hurt?" he said.

"I just need to clean myself up," she said. "You still haven't told me what you were doing there."

"Same thing you were, I suppose. Why did you want to hear what Escher had to say? What could he have to say that could possibly matter to you?"

"What's that supposed to mean?" She sounded a tad offended.

"Are you a pacifist?" said Bertram.

"A what?"

"I didn't think so. I doubted you even knew what the word meant."

She took a step back from Bertram.

She must have been standing so very close to the sack of lime when it hit, Bertram thought.

Then she said, "Bert, I don't think we should

see each other anymore."

That, Bertram wasn't prepared for. Suddenly he felt the boxed ring in his front pocket pressing his thigh and making a noticeable bulge. He tried to say something, but she responded as if he'd asked the obvious question.

"Because I just don't think it's working anymore," she said.

All Bertram could do was look at her with a dumb stare as Lucinda walked off, trailing white dust to some mysterious place inside the building.

There was nothing he could do then but go to his statistics class. He didn't feel like going. He actually felt like lying down and dying or maybe going for a nap on the subway tracks. But he went. He sat there unable to hear anything the professor had to say. He simply gazed ahead when he was asked a question.

Bertram avoided the cafeteria after that. But about a week later, he spotted Lucinda on the subway, her lids half over her eyes, sitting between two men with their faces buried in newspapers. She looked like she hadn't made it to bed the night before.

His mother's cousin, the jeweler, said he

couldn't possibly buy back the ring from Bertram, causing a major rift between his mother and the cousin that culminated in an explosive argument at the family's Passover Seder. It ended when the jeweler finally said he would buy the ring back.

Bertram had never mentioned Lucinda Gold to Walt. Nor had they talked about that day when, thankfully, a plummeting bag of lime managed to avoid directly hitting anyone. He was not sure it was worth the bother. In a way, he could have thanked Walt. Marrying Lucinda Gold would have been disastrous for him, and the whole affair left him in better shape to discern real love when it came along in the person of Gloria Steppet, who became his first wife (as well as with Jo, much later on).

Lucinda had been, however, in the back of his mind since he first struck up this friendship with Walt Escher. They had run into each other in the produce aisle of the local Gristedes. Jo's passing was still recent, and Walt too was suddenly wifeless again, though for a different reason. It turned out they lived just a block apart, and each found some solace in the other at a vulnerable time.

The door buzzer went off, disturbing Bertram's thought about his play in the cribbage game—he hadn't realized how much he was paying attention. Because of Walt's visits, the buzzing no longer alarmed Bertram. It did, however, worry him. He dreaded the return of Detective Hodges. This was part of the reason he was so permissive with Walt. He felt safer with him there in case the police ever did come back.

He asked at the intercom, but he always had trouble hearing through that contraption and Walt was no help there. He buzzed the person in and sat down at the table again.

After a soft couple of knocks, he opened the door to Colleen Castle standing there. She was carrying over her shoulder a black suit on a coat hanger covered with a see-through dry cleaner's bag. They stared in shock at one another. Bertram could tell his appearance had taken her aback. He was thinner, unshowered, stubble-faced. She looked older as well, despite a fresh hair coloring, which had a screaming, vivid quality that contrasted badly with the lines on her face.

She said, "Seeing as how you obviously failed to mention to Earl that his uncle died, I decided I better come into the city and tell him myself."

Bertram could not think of anything to say to her before she could add, "Where's Earl?"

"He's not here, Colleen."

"Where is he?"

"I couldn't say for sure."

"I'm tired of playing this game with you! I want to talk to my son!"

"I'm not stopping you! He's not here! See for yourself!"

She stormed past him, but halted at the sight of Walt. "I'm sorry," she said with no hint of apology in her voice. "I didn't know you had company."

Walt smiled, half-stood up, and sat down again still smiling.

She stalked on, the see-through bag rustling behind her. She poked her head into the tiny kitchen, then the two bedrooms and the bathroom. It was the first time she'd ever been in Bertram's apartment. She would never tell a soul, but she had driven past the address more than a few times over the years, curious to see what at least the building where her mother lived looked like. Once she parked in front and counted up seventeen stories just to see if someone happened to be in the window.

Now she stood stymied, like she couldn't understand why her mother and then her son preferred this cramped, dusty cell to being with her at the house in Crompaugue.

"It's like he knew I was coming," she said, not exactly out loud.

Colleen was a tall woman, but looked diminutive in the doorway between Earl's room and the living room. In profile Bertram thought she looked strikingly like Jo. They had the same longish forehead, the same high cheekbones, the same delicate lips.

Bertram began to take pity on her.

"Let me hang that up for you, Colleen," he said, taking the suit. As he hung it the closet, he made the introductions between Colleen and Walt.

"Why don't you sit down and have some coffee with us," Walt said.

"No, thank you."

"Please do. Then Bertram can tell you where he thinks Earl might be. I'd say she has a right to know, wouldn't you?"

"Walt!" Bertram cried.

"You know where he is?" Colleen said. "I knew

you were hiding something! I knew you were lying to me!"

"Are you trying to ruin everything for Earl?" Bertram said to Walt. "What's wrong with you?"

"Bert, you're starting to go overboard."

"You want to tell her?"

"She won't betray Earl's secret."

"How can you be so sure?"

"Bert, she's his mother."

Colleen looked at Walt, grateful that someone finally realized that her being Earl's mother counted for something. She was stirred that Walt actually assumed she had her son's best interest at heart like any mother would.

But if an NYPD detective couldn't get anything out of him, Bertram was damned if Colleen Castle was going to. He looked at his watch—it was almost time for the news, anyway—and then walked off to his bedroom, shutting the door behind him.

Walt jumped up and pulled out a chair for Colleen. She was reluctant, but sat down. She shook a cigarette from a pack of Benson & Hedges from her pocketbook. Walt jumped again to find her an ashtray. She also accepted a cup of coffee from him, black.

She said, "I know Earl's secret already."

"You do?"

"He's a fag. I know that."

"Really? Earl? Are you sure?"

"Oh I'm sure alright." A long flame jetted upwards from the lighter when she lit the cigarette. Walt studied the glowing tip. "So he's with someone, right?" Colleen said. "Some man? That's why he's not here? That's why he hasn't been here at all lately? That's what that the old Jew doesn't want to tell me?"

Walt did not contradict her. He was fascinated by how sure of herself she was.

"How do you know that about Earl?" he said.

"I know."

"Did he tell you that?"

She shook her head no. "It's stupid," she said. "He's so stupid. I turn on the television and all I ever hear about is this...disease. Queers are dropping like flies and he wants to be one of them?" She pushed the cigarette into the ashtray even though it was just half-smoked. "Not in my house. You wanna act stupid then you better go someplace else and do it where I don't have to look at it." She picked up her coffee.

"Is that what you told him?" Walt said.

"You better believe it," she said.

Walt was inclined to think certain things about a woman when he first laid eyes on her. Usually they were nice things, good things. When he first saw Colleen he thought she was not especially unattractive, and certainly in need of love. Mostly she needed to be understood by somebody. He thought he could be that somebody for her, even if only for a little while. But now he found his desire to do that lessening.

"I suppose if *he*"—she gestured toward the closed bedroom door—"really doesn't know how to get in touch with Earl, I don't know how I'm going to explain his absence at his uncle's funeral. Everyone will think it's my fault, I suppose. It's a shame." She packed up her lighter and her smokes and got up from the table. "I don't want to get stuck in traffic. I hate driving in the city."

Walt escorted her to the door and opened it for her.

With her gone, Walt knocked on Bertram's door. "Coast is clear." He poked his head in.

Bertram was lying on the bed with the TV

remote in his hand. He said, "Go away, Walt. Leave and don't come back. And don't forget your damn cribbage board."

"I didn't tell her anything," Walt said.

"You didn't? I thought you said she had a right to know?"

"I changed my mind."

They stared at the TV a few moments.

"Did you know she kicked Earl out of the house?" Walt said.

"No. Earl never told me that."

They stopped talking as the news came on and the Muni takeover was the lead story. Bertram sat up in bed. They both listened to how a Muni professor had walked out on the roof of the Fripp Academic Center and gave a defiant speech. Short as it may have been, they played only a brief excerpt.

"Sonia Rasmussen-Vell?" Bertram said. "Have you ever heard of her?"

"No," said Walt. "But that name...I wonder if she has anything to do with Peter Vell?"

"Who's that?"

"A historian I met a couple of times."

They stayed quiet until the end of the report.

Bertram, looking drawn, tossed the remote on the bed and laid down facing away from Walt. "God, I wish Earl would call."

"Come out and finish the game with me."

"No."

Walt sighed. "Bert, don't be stupid. At our age, there's no luxury about looking after yourself or not. You may get yourself into a hole you can't climb out of."

"Walt?"

"Yeah?"

"Go home."

Walt stood for a moment. Then he went out to the living room, collected his game, and left.

12

With the success of Rasmussen's speech, Earl knew that, in time, she would need to make another appearance. Earl was writing that speech now, on an old manual typewriter Isabel had scared up, by the light of the television. The clacking could be heard all up and down the corridors of the third floor. He was grateful for the work on which to focus. It drew him away from dwelling on what Isabel had told him about Calvin and Sonia being "together." Anytime he allowed himself to think about it for too long, his insides began to throb, his head began to swim and his knee began to ache again. The idea of Calvin with Rasmussen hurt more than his abandonment of the cause.

"You have the most interesting face when

you're concentrating, Walt. What I can see of it anyway. How can you write in such poor light?"

He looked up and Sonia was standing in the doorway with a flashlight. She had mostly stayed away from the office since her speech, preferring to bask in the admiration of the students in the building. Earl wished he had closed and locked the door.

"Do you know you grunt very softly when you're lost in what you're doing?" she said.

Sonia was deporting herself differently—with a nobly triumphal air—since she first came in off the roof days ago. She looked less frayed than she did when she appeared on television. Her greasy, stringy hair had been tied back. Her blouse was not quite so filthy and her skirt did not cling so aggressively to the bulges and folds of her body. Her glasses didn't sit crookedly on her face. Something had happened to her. She had come off that roof a changed person.

She came in and availed herself of an opened bag of stale potato chips.

"You have to admit, Walt," she said, "I did a pretty damn great job." Earl was the only one who had not told her so. Her attempt to pry a compliment out of him left him even less inclined.

She said, "What—no kind words?"

"You had great material."

"That's true. I can't believe Calvin wrote that. Believe me, I had him as a student…"

"That's not all you had him as," said Earl. It slipped out. He regretted it instantly, wishing to engage her as little as possible. He did not know how long he could go on disguising his identity from her.

"Excuse me?" Sonia said. "What is that supposed…"

"Calvin didn't write your speech. I did."

"I see. Then why did he go around telling everyone he wrote it?"

Earl didn't answer.

She said, "I guess there's things about Calvin nobody will ever understand."

Again Earl said nothing.

"I wish he was still here. I'd like to thank him for making me go out there."

Earl thought to himself that if Calvin was here right now he'd probably say, "I didn't make you do it. I asked you and you said yes."

"He was right about everything," she said.

"When I was out there, everything he said made sense to me all of a sudden. I really could be of help. I really could have something to say. And just maybe I really can save my job. Everything suddenly felt like it was going to be alright."

Earl said, "Yeah, Calvin predicts the future better than the Psychic Hotline. And no 1-900 charges."

"Sarcasm?" Sonia said. "Well at least you're talking to me. I was getting the impression for some reason that you don't like me." She crunched a chip and pieces of it fell from her mouth.

Earl ducked his head a little lower toward the typewriter. Out of the corner of his eye, he saw her slip a folded piece of paper from a pocket in her long skirt.

"I've written this," she said. "Maybe you could read it over. I think it's getting to be time for me to go out there again, and I've got some things I'd like to say."

"What?" said Earl.

"You know, just a few things from the heart."

She unfolded the paper and placed it on top of the typewriter since Earl showed no interest in taking it from her.

Even in the terrible light, Earl could easily make out the words. They started off in earnest imitation of the first statement but quickly fell into shameless score-settling, including an accusation that the History Department systematically held women back from promotion. She talked of having "the horse's bit of phallocentrism in my mouth." Earl absorbed the words quickly, finding them moronic, but all that really mattered was that they came from her.

He sat back in his chair, deeper into shadow.

"No fucking way," he said.

"Excuse me?" she said.

"There's no way you're reading anything out there that was written by you. We didn't come all this way just to have you fuck everything up."

"Who do you think you are?" Sonia said.

"Now what's going to happen is you're gonna shut up until I tell you otherwise. Then when you do open your mouth, you're going to say the exact words I tell you to and nothing else."

She squinted at him furiously. Then she seemed to pull back some. She parted her lips to speak, thought a moment, and said, "Earl? Earl Castle? Is that you?"

He never spoke to her in such a tone and using such language, though he had wanted to many times. Even so, she recognized his fury. She had never seen it this unsheathed, but she had felt it every time they were in the classroom together.

"What are you doing here?" she said. "Why are you using a fake name? And what were you doing holed up in here with Calvin all this time?"

He thought about what he should say. He even considered continuing to claim to be Walt. But he said, "My life is nothing I want to discuss with you."

"Hey, I'm all for that," she huffed. "I must say I'm surprised. I would never have figured you to be involved in anything like this."

"Well, we'll just have to add it to the long list of things you would never have figured."

She finally became incensed at his tone. "What I meant is that it's hard to believe that someone as selfish and self-centered as you would care about anything but yourself!"

"Don't act like you know me."

"But I do know you. Everyone else here may think you're someone else, but I know the truth."

She let the insinuations of that hang in the air a minute, though Earl behaved as though he couldn't care less.

"Is that what's going on here, Earl? Are you trying to keep your identity a secret? Are you hedging your bets in case the takeover fails? You are the calculating one," she said.

"And what about you?" Earl said. "What do you think everyone would say if they knew what a fraud you were? What if they knew that the university fired you and you're really not a faculty member at all?" She fell back a little.

Then she said, "You know of course that I don't need your permission to do anything. If I want to go out there and read my own statement—and maybe say whatever else that might pop into my head—there's nothing you can do to stop me."

With that, he picked up the bullhorn at the side of the desk and yanked out the battery. He opened the bottom drawer of the desk and tucked it away inside.

"I just stopped you," he said.

She snatched her statement back for herself and stormed out of the office.

Earl tried to turn his attention back to crafting

the second statement, but he had a hard time concentrating. He was sure she'd spread word of his real identity to everyone, though he was no longer sure if that even mattered at this point.

Forty-five minutes after she left, Sonia showed up at the door again. Earl cursed himself again for not shutting and locking the door.

"I just wanted to apologize for yelling," she said. "I know everyone here's under a lot of pressure."

Earl ignored her.

After a few minutes, she said, "You don't have to worry, Earl. I didn't tell anyone who you really are," she said.

Earl went on typing.

Still she would not go away. She said, "I think I know why you feel so hostile toward me." She didn't bother to wait for him to respond. "I should have given you an A on that paper, Earl," she said.

"But you didn't," Earl couldn't help but say, though he still didn't look at her.

"No, I didn't. And I'm sorry. I was too hard on you, Earl. But I knew you would get over it. I knew you'd keep going. You're still young enough to benefit from adversity. The age I am now—

tough times leave you weaker, not stronger."

"What you say now is inconsequential," said Earl. "What matters is what you did when you had the power."

But she still had one more confession to make.

"To tell you the truth, Earl...I never even read your paper."

He was unable to conceal his disgust.

"How could you do that? How could you grade a paper you never read?" he said, his voice almost trembling.

"I'm sorry, Earl. Like I said, I didn't know how serious you were about everything..."

"Forget me, what about you? Don't you have any self-respect?"

"I just had so much to do. I was overwhelmed. The tenure committee meeting was coming up. You have no idea what hoops they make you jump through..."

"I don't care about your excuses," Earl said.

"Maybe they are just excuses. Maybe the truth is I just didn't feel like reading it. Maybe it wasn't even the first time it happened either. Maybe everything you said about me was true. I'm just a rotten teacher." She said this without any reflection in her voice, as if she was stating a dry fact. "And everything I said about you turned out to be wrong. Obviously you do care about something other than yourself. Something bigger than yourself. I can see that you care. I can see what love has made you do."

"You've got it wrong."

"I know that you and Calvin are—were—involved."

"Don't talk to me about Calvin!" Earl said. "Not when you and he have been..." He cut himself off. There were words he didn't want to hear himself saying.

Sonia, however, understood. "There was never anything going on between me and Calvin, Earl. I know everybody is saying there was, but there wasn't!"

"You're a liar. You're just saying what you think I want to hear."

"Earl! Calvin is a very handsome young man. He could probably have whoever he wanted. What would he want with me?" And with that, she turned away and burst into tears.

Earl believed her. He really knew it all along, he thought. As he watched her wipe her face with the sleeve of her blouse, the fire in his blood died down. He picked up a roll of paper towels from under the desk and handed them to her. She took them without thanking him. She unrolled a bunch and buried her face in them.

"What a mess I am," she said. "Here you and everyone else are trying to do something good for other people and I'm here crying over my personal problems."

"You've helped," Earl admitted. "You did a good job reading that statement out there. You got the attention turned back to us. That's a lot." He took in a breath and let it out as a long, slow sigh. "And I wasn't in on this at all," he said. "I'm only here by mistake."

"But you're here."

"Not because I chose to be."

Sonia laughed a little. "Come on, Earl. This isn't a prison. People have left. Even Calvin left. You could have left too."

"No, I couldn't have..." He was still reluctant to have a heart-to-heart with the person who tried to destroy him.

For a long while, neither of them said anything. Then she stood up straight, as if she were steeling herself. She took from her pocket the folded sheet of paper.

When Earl saw it, he said, "Not this again."

"Earl, please let me have the battery for the bullhorn."

So it was all about getting the battery. It was all her pathetic attempt to charm him. No wonder she didn't get tenure.

"Forget it," he said.

"There are some things I want to say. And since I'm the one going out there, I'm the one with her face on TV, I think I have a right to say them."

"You don't have the right to anything."

She lunged for the drawer it was in but Earl merely blocked her with his legs. She tried to push him out of the way, but he did not have to hold to the desk very hard to prevent her from moving him.

She stood back, breathing hard, with her hand on her chest. She almost seemed like she was signaling something was wrong. Earl wondered if she might be having a heart attack, but somehow he did not buy it. After a minute she returned to breathing normally. She turned and walked out of the office.

Earl listened until footsteps disappeared. He was glad to find that, even after all they just revealed to each other, he didn't like her any more than he had before.

He worked for an hour or so more on the speech, which he felt confident Sonia Rasmussen would deliver when the time came. Then he decided to leave off on it, since the time for the afternoon news was approaching.

Isabel showed up with some food. "Where's Sonia?" she said.

"Who cares?" Earl said.

Isabel asked if she could stay and watch the news with him.

As they watched, he opened a can of ravioli from one of Calvin's stashes and ate it cold with a dirty plastic fork and a warm beer. "I appreciate that you brought me food," he said, "but I can't stand another peanut butter sandwich."

"Yeah, we should have thought that out better. I mean, there must be other things that are non-perishable."

At the very start of the broadcast, the news reader said they were going to go right to Municipal University in Harlem where it appeared as though something was going on.

The next picture they showed was a long shot of the very building Earl was in. The camera then zoomed to a small figure standing on the roof. It appeared to be Sonia and she appeared to be carrying a bullhorn.

"What is she doing?" Earl said. "That bullhorn doesn't even have a battery."

"Yes, it does," Isabel said. "I gave it to her, Walt. She came to me and said the old battery was dead. She asked if I could find another one. So I went around to the other maintenance rooms until I found that one."

"Goddammit!"

"Why are you so opposed to her going out there again to read her own words anyway? I read what she wrote. I think she made some good points."

"This isn't debate class! She's contaminating the purity of the cause!"

"Say what?"

"If she starts making all these irrelevant demands, she weakens the whole argument."

"Maybe it won't be that bad. Maybe you're overreacting."

Sonia looked different on TV than she had the first time. She had taken care to pin her hair back. And she appeared more confident. She had her statement out. She stalled for a moment. The wind flapped the paper in her hand. She looked behind her, as if to see if anyone had followed her to the roof, then swung forward again, suddenly losing her balance.

Then she fell.

Isabel gasped and covered her mouth.

The camera caught it all. Her plummet was almost artful, headfirst with her long skirt ruffling behind her. And though her landing could not be seen by the cameras because the grass sloped steeply downward as it neared the building, it was clear that hitting the ground in that particular way would be devastating.

"Oh, dear. Oh my. It appears we've witnessed a terrible, terrible event here..."

Earl and Isabel watched together silently. They saw the paramedics arrive. They saw them carrying Sonia away on a stretcher. She was covered in a white sheet up to her chin. It was impossible to tell if she was conscious or not, but she did not appear to be moving.

"Oh my God!" Isabel said.

"Don't panic!" said Earl. "Maybe it's not that bad. I mean, maybe she's not that hurt."

It may have been cold of Earl but he found himself wondering where Sonia's statement was. Was it sitting on the grass somewhere? Did some reporter pick it up? Would her words be put out there anyway?

Several minutes later, the newscaster said Sonia was dead.

Isabel bolted from her chair and ran out of the office. Earl got up and followed her out. She was already the length of the corridor away. He called, "Where are you going?"

She turned around but never stopped moving away. "It's over, Walt! Can't you see that?"

"No, it isn't! We can still do this! We can still win!"

She scrambled through the double doors and down the stairwell.

Earl went back to the office. He tried to get a hold of his reeling mind. He wondered how many of the others would react like Isabel. He tried to see his way to some logical next step.

He sat down at the desk. He closed his eyes.

"Calvin," he whispered. "You said you'd come back. Why did you leave me?" He covered his face and began to weep uncontrollably. He couldn't escape the idea that everything he allowed himself to believe in—The Great Plan, Calvin, the takeover—had disintegrated into dust. He had gone from one ridiculous, made-up conceit to another to another.

He kept hearing his mother tell him how stupid he was to think that anything could work out in his favor.

He had a sudden desire to talk to Bertram. He grabbed the phone receiver. Of course it was futile. Of course there was no dial tone. He slammed the receiver back down. Here he was again, still trying to will the impossible to happen.

Even as he watched Rasmussen falling, he was thinking that she'd be fine, she'd walk away from this, it didn't matter that that she was falling directly on her head from six stories up. The laws of gravity and human anatomy were nothing in the face of the will of the great Earl Castle. What an idiot he'd been.

He unspooled a stretch of paper towels and dried his face and hands.

Almost incidentally, he turned his head to the TV. It took him a moment to realize he was watching the police employ a battering ram against a door. He didn't know what door it was or even what building, but he was stunned when the door gave way and the police began pouring into the building.

In the wake of Rasmussen's death, it was clear. Enough was enough. They were in. And Earl had nowhere to go.

13

Along with Earl and much of the city, Bertram and Walt had watched the dramatic end of Sonia Rasmussen. Since then, the television had shown the fall over and over—in slow motion, stopped frame by frame, from different angles. There was a certain mercy in the fact that none of the cameras had been positioned to record her actual impact with the ground, though that didn't stop their filming of her lifeless body on the grass covered by a white sheet, her long ponytail sticking out one side like the tail of a scavenging fox.

After that, the announcements came in the chopped-up, breathless syntax of a TV reporter without a script from which to read:

...the police are in the building and have

entered the building at this time.

Two protesters were seen jumping from a second-story window of the second floor of the Fripp building and hitting on the grass and scrambling away.

Police have the confidence now that all the buildings have been emptied...

Some students were being led away in handcuffs. Bertram squinted at the television, but he could not see Earl among them.

The afternoon wore on to the evening. The police commissioner appeared at a news conference and said their investigation of Rasmussen's death was continuing, but that given what was visible on the videotape, they were working on the assumption that it was an accident.

Muni said most of the students involved would be given amnesty and that the semester would not be canceled. Instead, there would be an additional two weeks to wrap classes up, followed the next day by graduation.

But although Bertram waited and waited for Earl to come home or call, there was no sign of him at all. It left Bertram with a chilled feeling.

"Do you think we could have been wrong all this time, Walt?"

"Wrong about what?"

"About Earl being involved in the takeover. Maybe he was never in there in the first place."

"What about the phone call from Earl that the police traced?"

"Then where is he?"

"I don't know, Bert."

"Something terrible has happened to him. I know it." He put his hands on the side of his head. "They said most of the students would be given amnesty. That means a few of them won't be. The police or the school must have him. And that means it's all over for him. No scholarship, no nothing."

"You don't know that, Bert."

Over the next several hours, Bertram searched the phonebook and called hospitals and police stations. Still, he could not find Earl or even anyone who had heard of him. Bertram began to imagine all the terrible scenarios he could. With each one, Walt said, "Bert, you don't know that."

"It's a good thing you're here to tell me everything I don't know," Bertram snapped.

"Don't get sarcastic with me, Bert. If you don't want me here, all you have to do is say so."

"I just don't understand what you're doing here all the time!"

"If it wasn't for me, you'd have starved to death long ago!"

"And that's another thing! I've had so much Chinese food I'm shitting egg rolls. Haven't you ever heard of Thai or Mexican?"

"Excuse me for trying to help. I care about the kid too, you know. If I didn't, I would never have agreed to talk to Rhyman on his behalf."

"I'm surprised you can find the time off from chasing every skirt you see."

"Hey, it's not my fault if I have a big libido. That's the way God made me."

"And there's a long line of women who could testify to that, I'm sure."

"So who are you now? The Moral Majority?"

The truth was Bertram had always been somewhat disgusted by what appeared to be Walt's cavalier attitude toward love. Love, Bertram said, was never something to be treated so carelessly. He said, "I was actually rather appalled when you first told me you had been married and divorced no less than five times." Walt had admitted that to him with an unhappy smile that was still somehow tinctured by fond rememberings.

"I didn't plan it that way," Walt said, apparently feeling the need to defend himself. "I couldn't have known what was going to happen."

"Really? Even with the fourth or fifth one, you didn't look at the odds and say, 'Hmmm...'?"

"The odds?" Walt said. "I was in love with every single one of them! The odds? I was... trying for fulfillment! I wasn't calculating insurance premiums, for God's sake."

"Oh really? Were you trying for love and fulfillment with Lucinda Gold too?"

Walt sat back. He had a puzzled look on his face, which then gave way to "I don't know any Lucinda Gold."

"I'm sure you don't," Bertram said. "Our Muni days are a long way behind us at this point."

"Muni?" Walt said. "Wait a minute. Lucinda Gold?—That was also the color of her hair!"

"That's her."

"I haven't thought about Lucinda Gold in ages. Loose Lucinda"—he made a smacking sound in his mouth with his right cheek. "A bit of a dingbat, as I recall. But she sure knew what she was doing in the sack. Did you know her?"

"Well… a little…"

"Yeah, I think there were a lot of guys who Lucinda Gold knew 'a little'."

"Really? Are you sure about that?"

"Oh, yeah. She was with one of them when I first laid eyes on her—in the cafeteria, I think. Some poor sap who was not in her league at all. She was leading him around by the nose. She didn't even like him. She told me she only went out with him because she felt sorry for him."

Bertram searched Walt's face.

"You don't remember me," Bertram said. "Do you?"

"What? What are you talking about?"

"If you didn't remember me, then why did you act like you did when I came up to you at the Gristedes that day?"

Walt slid back in his chair and was silent for a good while.

"I guess I didn't want to be rude," he said eventually.

Bertram barely contained a laugh.

Walt went on, "You seemed to know who I was. And once you mentioned Muni, I figured we must have crossed paths at some time. It was nice talking to someone about the old Muni days. Everyone else I've lost touch with."

Bertram turned his head, embarrassed.

Walt went on, "And Karen had just left me. She was my last wife. I guess when I ran into you, I was, in a way, feeling a little alone."

Bertram thought of Jo and closed his eyes. At the time, she hadn't been long dead. Maybe that had something to do with his talking to Walt that day. He wasn't sure.

"Do you know what it's like to get left by five wives in a row?" Walt said.

Bertram opened his eyes. For the first time Walt didn't seem proud or amused by his string of women. "No, I don't," said Bertram.

Bertram laid back in the bed and rubbed his eyes. He was suddenly very tired.

"Where do you suppose Earl is?" he said.

It had been chilly all night.

Still, Earl slept. He was curled into a corner, behind an HVAC unit. The gravel kept pinching his arms and small of his back where his shirt hitched up, but in the end his exhaustion won out.

He had run to the roof, unable to think of anyplace else to go. He expected the police to eventually follow him there. But they didn't. An NYPD helicopter buzzed overhead a few times. He pulled a cardboard box over him. He laid as still as he had on the stack of gym mats in the maintenance room. It seemed so long ago now, but he still recalled everything Calvin had said and the sound of his voice as he said it.

When he awoke, he had no idea how much time had passed, but the dissipated blue and white of the sky gave him an impression of early morning. The sun appeared to be gaining altitude.

He crept to the roof wall and carefully peered over the side. The police cars and news crews were gone. The protesters were gone. A few workers were straggling in. They were sleepy-eyed and walked with gaits that suggested they weren't thrilled to be back. He felt vertigo and pulled back.

At his feet he noticed a piece of paper. It was Rasmussen's speech. He folded it and slipped it into his pocket.

He walked to the stairwell door and quietly

went inside. The first thing he noticed was that the lights in the stairwell were on.

He took the stairs all the way down and emerged on the first floor. The chains were gone from the doors. The brown paper on the glass wall had been torn away. Walking through the corridor, he thought the place looked more like its old self. But it was still eerie for the lack of people. He came to the set of double doors that led to the campus outside. He gently pushed the doors open and walked out into the open. The bricks looked like the color of rich earth in the early morning sun.

No one was there to see him. He walked down the hill to the subway station.

On the subway ride back to the apartment, people studiously ignored him. He could see why when he caught a faint reflection in the train window of his disheveled state. He spotted a copy of *The New York Post* crumpled under one of the seats. It was folded back, but he found the front page. There was Sonia, falling headfirst in a blur. The headline read MUNI PROTEST COMES CRASHING DOWN.

He arrived at the apartment building. He got on

the elevator and walked up to the apartment door. He wasn't sure why he felt as though he should knock. Instead, he used his key and let himself in.

The place looked just the same yet had a bare feeling to it. He wondered why the small black lamp on the desk was on in the daylight. He snapped it off.

"Bertram?" he called to no reply.

As he headed to his bedroom, he was stopped by the sight of himself in the hallway mirror. The sight confirmed what the train window had only hinted at. He was near unrecognizable.

He stripped off his clothes and headed straight for the shower. He ran the water so hot it turned his skin red. He scrubbed every part of his body, between his fingers and toes, the tips of his elbows. Then he rinsed and did it all over again. He shampooed his hair three times.

Still, when he was done, he thought he could smell Calvin a little in his beard. So he shaved it off.

He came out of the bathroom wrapped in his bathrobe, which he didn't remember feeling quite so soft.

He realized he was starving. He went to the

refrigerator, content to eat whatever was there, which was only some leftover Chinese takeout. He stuck it in the microwave for a minute and, really, it wasn't bad at all.

As he was eating, he noticed the mail that had piled up for him on the frosted vessel. He went through the stack; most of it was junk.

Then he came across the letter that had arrived from the Dean's office. It had been opened in a neat tear across the top of the envelope, the way Bertram opened all his own mail. Bertram's nosiness did not anger him as it always had before. Similarly, the news imparted by the letter did not thrill him the way he might have expected.

He slipped the letter back into its envelope. His stomach full, he felt very sleepy now. He retired to the comfort of his own bed in his own room.

He awoke a short time later to the sounds of shuffling in the apartment. He got out of bed and went to say hello to Bertram.

Only it wasn't Bertram who was knocking around. It was Walt.

"Earl!" he said.

"Hi, Walt."

"You're back!"

"Seems so."

Walt approached to embrace him. Earl stood stiffly. Walt had never been so demonstrative toward him before. He had always regarded Earl with a respectful but frank distance, like one would a scorpion.

"I can't believe what you did!" Walt said. "You kids really gave 'em hell, didn't you?"

"Did we?" Earl said. He shook some clarity into his head. "Did they rescind the tuition hike?"

"Well, no, not that I've heard."

"Did they back down on the layoffs or the financial aid?"

"Earl…"

"So we failed on every demand. Not to mention that a person is dead. Is that what you call giving them hell?"

"That wasn't your fault, Earl. They're calling that an accident. Hell, the whole city saw on TV how she was on that roof alone and slipped. And as for your demands, you still don't know what's going to happen. And at the very least, you called attention to issues that nobody cared about before."

Earl watched him as he spoke. Walt believed

the things he was saying. Earl thought about telling him how he'd assumed his name in a state of panic. Walt would probably have been greatly amused.

"I have to say, though," Walt went on, "that I would never have expected that you of all people would be involved in something like this."

Earl fell silent.

"I guess nobody really knows you all that well. Huh, Earl?" Walt said.

Earl had to wonder what that meant. He had never discussed his sexuality with Walt or Bertram. It didn't seem worth the trouble and it went against his natural reticence. But he wouldn't be surprised if they both knew. He never went to any lengths to hide it. He never faked sexual interest in women. One time, not long after Earl first moved in, Bertram was sitting in his recliner engrossed in a newspaper story when he muttered to himself, "What a *fagelah*."

"What a what?" said Earl, who was within earshot.

"Oh. It's an old Yiddish word."

"Meaning what?"

"A tutti frutti."

Earl could tell the old man was not talking about ice cream.

After that, the topic was never brought up again. Earl viewed it as a tacit agreement. For Bertram's part, it wasn't hard to avoid talking about something he never gave two shakes about.

"Where is Bertram?" Earl said to Walt.

"Columbia Presbyterian."

"What? Why? What happened?"

"They're not sure. I found him passed out on the floor when I came over this morning. It was strange. He gave me his key last night. It was like he knew something was going to happen. I just came back to get all his medications. The doctors need to know everything he's taking."

"Is he going to be alright?"

"I don't know. But he hasn't been taking very good care of himself since you disappeared. He's been very worried about you."

Earl had no idea Bertram would react that way.

"You better come back to the hospital with me. They won't tell me very much. They say it's because I'm not a relative. But they'll tell you."

Earl was going to say that, no, he wasn't Bertram's relative at all, but he didn't.

When he got to the hospital and the doctor asked him who he was, he said, "I'm his grandson," and for the first time he felt it to be true.

Bertram looked bloodless and somehow flattened against the hospital bed. His face in particular seemed to have lost all of its contours. Earl tried not to show how taken aback he was. A stack of machines whirred and hiccupped at his bedside, including one that let out an incessant beep.

He was conscious and even managed a smile when he saw Earl walk in. "Earl," he said, his voice a fragile rasp, "Look at you. You look even thinner than before."

"I'm not the only one," Earl said. "I never meant to upset you, Bertram."

"This isn't your fault, Earl. It's mine for taking such poor care of myself all these years. I'm just glad you're okay. You are okay, aren't you?"

Earl nodded.

"You really did surprise me, Earl. I had no idea that you were planning to take over the school like that. I didn't think you cared about that kind of thing."

"It was kind of a surprise for me, too."

Earl was about to discover a kind of cachet associated with people who were part of the takeover.

"It must have been quite an experience," Bertram said.

Earl knew he was trying to ask him to tell him all about it. But he stayed quiet, deciding the mystery of it was enough.

"I was most worried about what it might do to your plans—your goals. Have you been to the apartment yet, Earl?" Bertram said.

Earl nodded again.

"Then you know about the letter?"

"Yes."

"Do you think your involvement in the takeover might cause them to pick a different valedictorian?"

"I don't know."

"Well congratulations anyway, Earl. Even if they end up taking it away from you, you'll always know you were able to do it."

"I suppose so."

"And I'm sorry for opening your mail again, Earl."

"Don't be."

The doctor came in then. He was a small, thin man with a big swoop of graying hair that reached down his forehead almost to his eyes. His expression was kindly, if distracted. He did a few checks of the equipment to which Bertram was hooked up, all the while asking the patient how he felt. Within a few minutes he was out the door again. Earl said, "I've got to find a bathroom," but he followed the doctor and stopped him, explaining that he was Bertram's grandson. "What happened to him?" he said.

The doctor said Bertram had suffered a major heart attack. "As far as we can figure, it had happened several days ago."

"How is that possible?" Earl said.

"It happens. People can have heart attacks without even knowing it. People can put up with a lot of pain when they don't realize it's not normal. He's very lucky to have survived this long."

"So what's the prognosis?"

"There's a lot of damage to his heart muscle," was all the doctor would say.

For the next three days, Earl stayed at Bertram's side. The one time he went home was to shower and change clothes. He noticed the light on the answering machine flashing madly. He ignored it.

The chair he sat in in the hospital room was very uncomfortable, but Earl stayed even though Bertram spent a good part of the time asleep. Walt paid for a television to be wheeled in, and that gave them something to look at together. When night came, Earl asked if he could stay and the nurse allowed it, though she said she was breaking the rules by doing so. Walt dropped by several times a day with Chinese food. They were the only two visitors Bertram had.

The TV had mercifully little to say about the takeover, having moved on to the search for a man who pushed another man in front of a subway train at the Columbus Circle station. About all Earl heard was the students involved in the takeover would not be expelled, but instead put on some sort of probation. Earl thought of Calvin and his knack for evading consequences.

At one point, Bertram opened his eyes suddenly. "Earl," he said, "you don't have to stay with me."

Earl shook his head vigorously, as if to free

himself of any possibility of leaving.

Bertram smiled and closed his eyes again.

The waiting reminded him of all the hours he spent sitting in Calvin's office, waiting for something to happen, believing that something would, that the world would change, that Calvin would walk through the door, that love would see them through. But now he felt the flat, affectless, utterly pointless passage of time.

Classes at Municipal University were finished up in a rough and hurried fashion over the next two weeks. Rasmussen's class was taken over by the History Department chair, who was well aware of Earl and had no problem giving him his A.

Naturally there was discussion about Rasmussen at the start of the first class back. Calvin seemed to have been right about her the whole time. She had become something of a revered figure among the students. One student blubbered a little. Another recounted how she devoted so much extra time to him, and how he wouldn't have passed were it not for her. Earl was a little surprised to find that the students in the class seemed to be fond of her. Of course, the fact that she was dead had a way of making her seem not so bad.

But he did wonder a bit about his lack of sadness regarding her passing. She had been a pain in the ass to him from the day he met her to the last hour of her life. And she was the only one other than Calvin who had known his real name and who was likely to spread it around that the valedictorian of the Municipal University of New York graduating class of 1988 was there and deeply involved in the takeover. But he never wished for anything like this to happen.

More than a few times he thought about seeing if Calvin was around, but then thought better of it. Once, though, he could not resist walking by his office. It was closed, locked, with the lights out.

He was thankful that the last two weeks of classes kept him occupied with a flurry of test-taking and paper-writing. The last day of classes was followed the very next day by a hasty graduation.

Earl's valedictory speech, written over several frantic, feverish nights, went through many drafts. At first, he avoided the takeover altogether, focusing instead on AIDS and how everyone must keep a place in their heart for those who suffer. But he realized the noble intentions of the protesters had to be acknowledged. He did not mention anyone by name.

He wished Bertram could have been there. He wished he could tell him that he really was grateful, despite the many times he had wished the old man would go away.

Toward the end of the graduation ceremony, the college president, a woman Earl had never met before, said a few words.

"We have been trying to think of a way to honor the memory of our fallen colleague," she said. "We have decided to set up the Sonia Rasmussen-Vell Memorial Scholarship. It's a small, one-thousand dollar award given to the top history or political science student of the year. That, of course, is our valedictorian. So it gives me pride to award the first Sonia Rasmussen-Vell Award to Earl Castle."

Earl was a little flabbergasted. He had not been told of this beforehand. He was now expected to say a few words about her.

"Sonia Rasmussen-Vell was a professor of mine. I feel I learned some valuable things from her. I'm sorry about what happened to her. We never meant for anything like that—I mean, we never expect someone to be taken away from us like that."

He looked over at the President, the Dean and all the other officials gathered on the stage and thought they were regarding him rather strangely. Afterward, as he said his goodbyes to them, he thought the same thing. He wondered if they would have even cared that he was involved in the takeover.

On that day he walked away from Muni and did not look back. That was how it should be, he imagined Bertram saying.

The next day Earl learned he'd won the Rhyman Scholarship. He received a phone call from the chairman of the foundation, George Rhyman, who said he was the oldest son of Marcus Rhyman.

"It's spectacular!" George Rhyman said. "It's two years in Europe. It's four world capitals. Rhyman fellows have gone on to some great things, Earl! Positions in the Ivy League, at the White House. This is an opportunity like you'll never get again in a lifetime."

"I understand that. And it's awfully nice, Mr. Rhyman. But I can't go."

George Rhyman went silent on the line.

"My grandfather, he fell sick," Earl said. "I can't leave him right now."

Daniel Scott

PART III

May 21, 1988

Daniel Scott

14

Walt and Earl were packing up some things in Bertram's apartment. Earl was in his room putting his books into boxes when a tentative knock came at the door. Walt peered through the peephole. It was a strange black man. Walt would never admit it to anyone, but he was apprehensive about opening the door. Still, he knew that was a very old prejudice on his part, and he wasn't about to let that start dictating his actions at this late stage. He unlocked the door and opened it.

"Hi," the black man said. "Does Earl Castle live here?"

"Do you know him?"

"Yeah. I'm, ah, a friend of his."

"Really? A friend of Earl's?"

"I'm Calvin Reynolds. I knew Earl from Muni.

He stuck his hand out and Walt paused before he shook it. Calvin noticed the pause but did his best to put the old man at ease by flashing that winning smile. "You must be Earl's—let's see—his former step-grandfather?"

"Well…"

"Earl told me all about you. I think he thought I wasn't listening, but I was."

"Actually, Earl's grandfather died about a week ago," Walt said. "We were just starting to clear out his things."

Suddenly Earl emerged from his room with a box of books. He halted at the sight of Calvin. It was the first he'd seen of Calvin since he disappeared during the takeover. The rush he had always felt at the sight of him swelled inside him. The wrinkles around Calvin's eyes were deeper than they were before, but if anything that enhanced his handsomeness.

"Calvin," Earl said, almost unconsciously.

It didn't take long for Walt to figure out they needed to be alone. He invited Calvin in and then said he was going to start going through Bertram's bedroom closet, and he disappeared into that room.

Calvin moved toward Earl and Earl allowed himself to be kissed.

"How are you, Earl?"

"I'm alright."

"I heard you got what you wanted. Congrats."

"Thanks. How did you find out where I lived?"

"Oh, you know, it wasn't hard. All it took was a peek at the right file."

Earl recalled Calvin's infinite connectedness at Muni.

Calvin said, "I'm enrolled again. For the summer. Two classes. So in the fall I'll have 85 credits."

"You need 120 to graduate."

"I know. But I think I can do it this time. I can feel that things are different now."

"I guess Rasmussen's death affected us all."

"It wasn't that." Calvin took Earl by the hands. "It was you, Earl."

Earl was wordless until finally he said:

"I waited for you."

"Yeah, I know."

"But you never came back."

Calvin looked away.

"You said you were coming back. But you just

left me there instead."

"I know, but it all worked out, didn't it?"

Earl pulled his hands away. He felt the familiar pain whenever he refused something from Calvin.

"Why are you here?" Earl said.

"Because I missed you. I wanted to see you. I wanted to tell you the time we had together… meant a lot to me."

Earl smiled.

"I was hoping maybe sometime we could go for coffee. Or a cigarette."

"Well, this is a really bad time," Earl said. I mean, I just came from a funeral and there's all this stuff that we're clearing out."

"I know. How about you come over to my place tonight?" Calvin took out a pen and wrote the address on the back of a book of matches. "I'll fix us something to eat. We can talk. Okay?"

Earl looked at the address. It was somewhere in Washington Heights.

"Let's say seven o'clock, okay?" Calvin said.

"Okay," said Earl. Before Calvin left, he embraced Earl. It was only a second before Earl stopped resisting and allowed himself to be taken over by those strong arms once again. Despite everything, he missed Calvin too. In the embrace, Calvin maneuvered Earl's hand over his crotch. Calvin was already half-aroused.

"That misses you too," Calvin smiled.

It took a couple more hours for Earl and Walt to finish cleaning out the apartment. The furniture —the desk, the bookcases, Bertram's recliner— was all left, to be taken away later by movers.

Earl had turned strangely silent since the visit from his friend. He didn't respond when Walt said, "I'm glad you made at least one friend at Muni."

They packed everything into the car Walt had rented for the purpose. Then they got in the front.

"Well, you ready?" Walt said.

Earl nodded. "I want to thank you for everything, Walt."

"Hey, you deserved it. You earned it."

It was Walt who helped Earl postpone the Rhyman scholarship so he could be there through Bertram's illness and eventual death. Earl was, after all, the only family Bertram had.

Walt put the car in gear and they drove to the airport. Earl had a 6:30 flight to Prague.

Daniel Scott

About the Author

Daniel Scott is the author of two books of fiction, *Some of Us Have to Get Up in the Morning* and *Pay This Amount*. He is the recipient of various grants and fellowships from sources such as the Christopher Isherwood Foundation, the New York Foundation for the Arts, and the MacDowell Colony. Born and raised on Boston's South Shore, he currently lives in New York City.

Visit the author's website at
http://www.danielscottonline.com

If you enjoyed *Valedictory,* consider these other fine books from Savant Books and Publications:

Essay, Essay, Essay by Yasuo Kobachi
Aloha from Coffee Island by Walter Miyanari
Footprints, Smiles and Little White Lies by Daniel S. Janik
The Illustrated Middle Earth by Daniel S. Janik
Last and Final Harvest by Daniel S. Janik
A Whale's Tale by Daniel S. Janik
Tropic of California by R. Page Kaufman
Tropic of California (the companion music CD) by R. Page Kaufman
The Village Curtain by Tony Tame
Dare to Love in Oz by William Maltese
The Interzone by Tatsuyuki Kobayashi
Today I Am a Man by Larry Rodness
The Bahrain Conspiracy by Bentley Gates
Called Home by Gloria Schumann
Kanaka Blues by Mike Farris
First Breath edited by Z. M. Oliver
Poor Rich by Jean Blasiar
Ammon's Horn by Guerrino Amati
The Jumper Chronicles by W. C. Peever
William Maltese's Flicker by William Maltese
My Unborn Child by Orest Stocco
Last Song of the Whales by Four Arrows
Perilous Panacea by Ronald Klueh
Falling but Fulfilled by Zachary M. Oliver
Mythical Voyage by Robin Ymer
Hello, Norma Jean by Sue Dolleris
Richer by Jean Blasiar
Manifest Intent by Mike Farris
Charlie No Face by David B. Seaburn
Number One Bestseller by Brian Morley
My Two Wives and Three Husbands by S. Stanley Gordon
In Dire Straits by Jim Currie
Wretched Land by Mila Komarnisky
Chan Kim by Ilan Herman
Who's Killing All the Lawyers? by A. G. Hayes
Ammon's Horn by G. Amati
Wavelengths edited by Zachary M. Oliver
Almost Paradise by Laurie Hanan
Communion by Jean Blasiar and Jonathan Marcantoni
The Oil Man by Leon Puissegur
Random Views of Asia from the Mid-Pacific by William E. Sharp
The Isla Vista Crucible by Reilly Ridgell
Blood Money by Scott Mastro
In the Himalayan Nights by Anoop Chandola
On My Behalf by Helen Doan
Traveler's Rest by Jonathan Marcantoni

Valedictory

Keys in the River by Tendai Mwanaka
Chimney Bluffs by David B. Seaburn
The Loons by Sue Dolleris
Light Surfer by David Allan Williams
The Judas List by A. G. Hayes
Path of the Templar: The Jumper Chronicles Book 2 by W. C. Peever
The Desperate Cycle by Tony Tame
Shutterbug by Buz Sawyer
Blessed are the Peacekeepers by Tom Donnelly/Mike Munger
Purple Haze by George B. Hudson
The Turtle Dances by Daniel S. Janik
The Lazarus Conspiracies by Richard Rose
Imminent Danger by A. G. Hayes
Lullaby Moon by Malia Elliott of Leon & Malia
Volutions edited by Suzanne Langford
In the Eyes of the Son by Hans Brinckmann
The Hanging of Dr. Hanson by Bentley Gates
Written in the Stars - An Anthology edited by Sabrina Favors
Flight of Destiny by Francis H. Powell
Elaine of Corbenic by Tima Z. Newman
Ballerina Birdies by Marina Yamamoto
More More Time by David B. Seaburn
Crazy Like Me by Erin Lee
Cleopatra Unconquered by Helen R. Davis

Coming Works
All Things Await by Seth Clabough
Big Heaven by Charlotte Hebert
Captain Riddle's Treasure by GV Rao Rama
Tsunami Libido by Cate Burns
The Chemical Factor by A. G. Hayes
Quantum Death by A. G. Hayes
The Adventures of Purple Head, Buddha Monkey and Sticky Feet by Eric Bracht

http://www.savantbooksandpublications.com